In memory of
Albert and Marian Cartwright,
and Roberta Allen.

'Our task is to stamp this provisional, perishing earth into ourselves so deeply, so painfully and passionately, that its being may rise again 'invisibly' in us.'

Rainer Maria Rilke
On Being and the Transitory

NEPTUNE

Dorothy Browning

Taffy

July 11th 1947

To you the stars,

narcissi fields,

and music.

Peter

I can't remember when I first found Dorothy's grave. The trees were in blossom so it would have been springtime but beyond that I have no idea. I can't even remember whether I had met Bill or not by then. My guess is, probably not. But really it is all a blur. I wasn't much of a record keeper before I became an astrologer. Of course, now that I am an astrologer, it frustrates me intensely to think that among my hundreds of charts of every description, I haven't got the one for the all-important moment of discovering Dorothy's grave. I've got Birth Charts, Death Charts, Horaries and Decumbitures; charts for missing persons, errant spouses and misdirected mail. But have I got the one which I, personally, need, in order to make sense of it all? No;

therefore I will have to make do with what my Aquarian friend, Annie, would call, 'conditional reality' – with what actually happened.

What happened was this.

One day, while wandering in my local churchyard, I came across the long-neglected grave of Dorothy Browning. I imagine I must have been feeling rather empty at the time because I do remember, very vividly, the sensation, while standing on the grave, of being filled-up. Not with joy, or love, or wonder; or anything I can define; but with a kind of warm sympathy – a bit like taking a warm bath only on the inside. It rose from the earth through my feet, this warmth, spreading throughout my body until I was full, whereupon it flowed out and I flowed with it, out and across and into everything in the churchyard. That's the best I can do with words because there were no words in it, only feeling. Quite where I went after that, I have no idea. I simply stood there, taking it all in, until I was full, and then I flowed out: I only became aware of time and place as, very gradually, I came round.

This felt rather like being inside a photograph during the developing process: the trees, headstones, church tower, foliage; my feet, bare legs and plump hands emerging as through a film of oily liquid: various greens, greys, ochres and umbers separating and clarifying until, at last, I recognised my surroundings and began rubbing myself down.

I had in mind an image of Aladdin, rubbing the lamp to release the genie; only I was rubbing myself back in. I rubbed my feet, calves, thighs, knees and elbows; the tops of my arms, the front of my chest and the back of my neck. I then walked round the grave a few times, stopping to read the inscription again, this time, critically: -

Dorothy Browning. Taffy. July 11th, 1947. To you the stars, narcissi fields and music. Peter.

Hmm, I'll bet they weren't married, I thought. There was none of the usual, 'Beloved Wife and Mother Of.' No, they were lovers rather than spouses; and she had died young.

I could see Dorothy; a young, dark-haired woman with Celtic good looks, small feet and large eyes. Peter, I couldn't imagine at all. I had never met the kind of man who could express feelings poetically: well, not to me at any rate; but I had met lots of soulful Welsh women. Indeed, I was even related to some of them. So, Dorothy, 'Taffy', yes, I could picture her: small-boned, dark-haired, blue-eyed, pretty. Not stylish or fashionably dressed. Her skirt would have been a fraction too straight for the post-war, 'New Look;' her stockings not quite sheer enough, though she may have favoured slightly impractical shoes and would always have worn a hat. Nothing too extravagant, mind you: she wouldn't have wanted to draw attention to herself; for although she had plenty of spirit (she'd left home, after all, in dangerous times) she wasn't bold. And, besides, she would never have forgotten her mother's warnings on the subject of Vanity, even though, in her innocence, she would not have understood where it might lead.

That Dorothy had been an Innocent, I felt quite sure. Why else would Peter have desired for her, the stars, narcissi fields and music? No, she had been an Innocent Abroad, compelled by the exigencies of wartime to leave her beloved homeland, and it had all proved too much for her sensitive constitution: she had wasted away and died. And nothing - not even a love as strong as Peter's - held the power to save her.

Again, I can't remember how long I stood there, marvelling at the quality of this love, although I do recall wondering whether anyone would ever love me as deeply. I may even have wished for it, albeit without much conviction: I'd have been hard-pressed, in those days, to put my whole heart and soul into a wish. No, I expect I whispered it, hoping that it might come true while thinking that it probably wouldn't, for although I had always been a Great Believer in Love, I'd never quite managed it myself.

Nowadays, of course, I have the benefit of knowing that Venus, in my Birth Chart, is somewhat, 'afflicted,' let's say, by nebulous Neptune, but in those days, I could only think I was doomed because I was a bungler. Never in the right place at the right time, I was always having incongruous encounters overseas: - the Parisian artist, for one, who'd invited me to come up and behold his latest works, turned out to be a painter and decorator.

'Well, what do you think?' he asked, opening the studio apartment doors to reveal four walls painted white with a hint of apricot.

Then there was the Serbian student who revived me after a rucksack (with kettle attached) fell onto my head on a train bound for Athens. Ah, I can see him now: his magnificent cheekbones and tortured expression. For two years, we wrote every week until his letters and my address book mysteriously vanished.

Equally baffling was the sudden disappearance of my daughter's father, a Pisces. We had just moved in to live together when he announced he must follow his dream wherever it might lead; and was last heard playing guitar on a cruise ship bound for the Canaries.

Yes, well; no wonder I got the idea that love wasn't something I could quite pin down; and this wasn't something I changed my mind about either, as a result of my experience in the churchyard that day. I didn't come away from Dorothy's grave inspired by the new belief that love wasn't beyond me after all. I didn't come away feeling any differently from the way I had always felt. Something weird had happened. I didn't understand it. I was baffled. So I went home and ate my tea.

Looking back, I don't recall making a conscious decision to adopt Dorothy's grave. It just so happened that over the next few years, whenever I had an hour or two to spare (which wasn't often) I would go down to the churchyard and tidy things up a bit: cutting back brambles, pulling up bindweed and trimming the overhanging branches of trees. Usually, I was busy on the grave itself, but every now and again, I would sit myself down on a neighbouring plinth to relax and enjoy whatever spectacle the churchyard had to offer; for there was usually something untoward, if not downright illegal, going on within its bounds.Situated, as it is, in the heart of Oxford's 'Bohemian Quarter,' the churchyard provided something of a recreation ground for residents and transients alike. Sisters of Mercy, elderly couples, single mothers, juvenile delinquents: here they would come from all walks of life to stroll, browse, ruminate and congregate; to walk their dogs, feed stray cats, burn their rubbish and bury a well-loved family pet. Drug-dealers, law-enforcers, hardened-drinkers, power-walkers - you even got the occasional member of the Church of England passing through.

Come to think of it, I may even have spotted Bill in there once (though this was not how we met) demolishing a dry stone wall with his pickaxe and carting huge chunks of it across the main road in his wheelbarrow (I later discovered he was building a pond). About the only person I did not see in the churchyard in those days was the vicar.

One evening, I decided to go and smoke the vicar out, as it were. I had been doing some weeding on Dorothy's grave, and was just thinking about calling it a day, when it occurred to me that the vicar might know something about Dorothy and Peter. After all this was no ordinary inscription; and, for all I knew, their story could well have become a local legend. So, brushing myself free of twigs and scraping the mud off my boots, I ran my fingers through my hair, gathered up my tools, and headed off in the direction of the New Rectory.

Passing the old one as I went, I felt rather sorry that the Church appeared to have abandoned it. This New Rectory felt cold to me: cold and modern; which, I have to say, was also my impression of the vicar. Throughout our interview, he kept me standing on the threshold while he maintained a resolute grip on the half-open door, shunting it forwards an inch or so each time he answered a question.

No, the name Browning did not ring a bell; he was not aware of this particular grave.

Yes, I had clearly experienced something unusual in the churchyard; but thank you, no, he did not want a copy of the inscription.

Yes, the Church kept records, but he couldn't let me in to see them without an appointment. And, besides, that particular parish register was no longer kept in the church.

There now remained between us about five fraught inches of space, and I was sorely tempted to stick my foot into it but he closed the door before I could make a move after wishing me a terse, 'Good Evening.'

As I returned along the gravel driveway, I felt a mixture of disappointment and anger. Frustrated in my wish to share what I had experienced on Dorothy's grave with someone I hoped might be able to explain it for me, I also felt angered by the vicar's indifference and lack of Charity. He might have thought me a crank, but at least he could have offered me a cup of tea, and I cursed him under my breath as I slammed the gate soundly on the New Rectory and its incumbent.

'You won't catch me in here again,' I growled, 'not even at Christmas.'

But before long, I was happily eating a chocolate bar and talking myself out of my feelings. Maybe I wasn't meant to find out about Dorothy. Maybe it wasn't important, or the time wasn't right. After all, didn't I have quite enough to do already without taking on a research project to boot? No, I should leave well alone, I decided; and by the time I arrived home, had more or less managed to push Dorothy to the back of my mind. Oh, I continued to visit her grave from time to time, calling round on her anniversary with a bunch of flowers, but many years would pass before circumstances conspired to arouse my interest in her story again; prompted, this time, by beings of an altogether more worldly nature: my mother and Bill.

You'll forgive me, I hope, since we are still under the aegis of boundless Neptune; planet of true compassion, heartfelt sympathy and redemption through long-suffering, if I take a little time to meander in the mysterious realms of my relationship with Bill, trusting that it is all for a higher purpose.

I first met Bill during the autumn of 1992 (for me, a Saturn transit; for him, a blind date) and was immediately struck by a quality in his aura like heavy water. I did not know then, of course, that his Pluto conjoined my Ascendant, but it still felt fated. Having said this, it did not appear destined to last and, after a few months, we went our separate ways only to meet up again some four years later outside the local supermarket. By this time I had taken up Astrology while he had taken up with a beautiful and brilliant mathematician who had left him, he was sorry to report, after two years, for the City of London.

'The whole of it?' I asked incredulous.

'The Banks,' came his reply. 'What else do you do with an Oxford Degree these days? It's where the money is.'

'Well, I'm sorry to hear that, Bill,' I said, and muttered something about there not being too much money in Astrology - with or without a degree.

'In what?' It was his turn to look amazed.

'In Astrology. That's what I'm doing these days.'

'You were a History teacher the last time I looked.'

'I still am,' I replied. 'But I managed to reduce my hours so I can get on with my Astrology. I really love it. It's another language. Great fun.'

He nodded sagely. 'You've had a breakdown then since we last met. Oh, well, you probably needed one.'

'Oh, I don't think I have,' I replied cheerfully. 'Well, not so I noticed. Mind you, I'm a lot less anxious nowadays. And I've stopped switching the electricity off at the mains before I leave the house.'

'Ah, but have you stopped putting the alarm clock on the stove before you go out?'

'I have indeed.'

'And what about your endearing habit of wearing wellington boots in bed when lightning strikes?'

I smiled, 'Yes, I've stopped all that as well. I still pull out the plugs, of course – but not in other people's houses.'

'Your social life will have improved then.'

'I don't know about that, Bill; I'm far too busy for a social life. But I must say, I'm surprised that you remember my endearing nocturnal habits after all this time.'

'Oh, come now, Gwendolen,' he chided. 'How on earth could I have forgotten those? Really, you always manage to make it sound as though your habits are perfectly normal, and that you, yourself, are a singularly unexceptional member of the average population whereas, in fact, you are quite mad.'

'No, I'm not,' I replied, 'I'm normal. I'm a very normal person with traditional values.'

'You think so, do you?' He grinned as he lit a cigarette. 'Of course, most compulsives tend to find their condition is improved by a course of therapy or drug treatment but that wouldn't be normal enough for you. No, you find a remedy in Astrology, which proves it - you are mad. Not that I'm knocking it. If it works for you, fair enough.'

'I didn't say Astrology cured me of my habits,' I put in irritably. 'But, no, don't knock it, Bill, because it does work in my experience, although in rather mysterious ways.'

'Is that so?'

'Yes.' I replied emphatically, pulling out my Pocket Ephemeris, and pointing out that the sudden ending of his love affair had coincided with a transit of disruptive Uranus to his Venus in Aquarius - but not to worry because he could now look forward to a Jupiter Return.

'And that's good news, is it?'

'Yes. Well, you know, Jupiter, Father of the Gods. It's meant to be a time of opportunity and expansion.'

'Oh yes? Only you don't sound too sure.'

'No, I'm never too sure about Jupiter transits to be honest. I had Jupiter transiting my Sun when my father died which was hardly my idea of an opportunity. Far from it.'

'Oh, but it was. It surely was.' He took another pull on his cigarette while pausing for thought. 'Hmm, presumably it's up to the individual how they take these opportunities?'

'I suppose so,' I replied.

'And I've got Jupiter, you say?'

'That's right, you have.'

'In that case, I shall take advantage of this opportunity and invite my astrologer out to dinner.'

So, that was that: reunited under the auspices of Jupiter and a Progressed New Moon. And it was good, very jovial and expansive, for quite some time: we went punting; we went on picnics; we went out for meals. He even took me to dinner in College once. As for the longer term, I remained unsure; and it didn't help that lacking his time of birth, I couldn't erect his full Horoscope in order to compare it with mine. This annoyed me no end, as I'm sure you can imagine; though I got enormous pleasure out of speculating what Bill's Ascendant might be.

Could it be Leo (like mine) he was certainly flamboyant enough in public. Or Pisces (for such a tall man, he had unusually small feet). Or even Capricorn (he sat with his shoulders hunched). Astrologer friends declared in favour of Scorpio, alerted, no doubt, by his penetrating gaze and enigmatic expression. But I still had my doubts. I preferred Sagittarius: sign of the Philosopher (the Archer Aims his Bow towards the Heavens) though a story he once told me – and which really captured my imagination – suggested Gemini, sign of the Twins.

He had the vague idea, he once told me, that he had not been alone in the womb, but that his twin had died early on in the pregnancy before his mother even knew that she was pregnant. He had read somewhere that this could happen. Indeed, he had made a mental note of the facts:

'Seventeen per cent of embryos start off as twins,' he announced, 'which means, of course, that one in five of us are killers.'

'That's rather a grim way of looking at the statistics, isn't it,' I replied - after I finally managed to tot them up. 'How do you know your twin didn't just give up the ghost and die of her own accord? She could have taken a quick look out and thought: sod this for a game of soldiers, I'm staying put. Or she may have got the wrong century. Either way, it wouldn't mean you killed her.'

'Indeed. And that is not what I meant. But how do you know, I wonder, that my twin was a she?'

That threw me. 'Er, well, I don't, Bill, of course; but regardless of gender, what do you think your twin would have been like?' I asked this, I'm sure, half-hoping to receive a list of characteristics I could happily claim as my own: kind-hearted, absent-minded, creative, perhaps? But he wouldn't be drawn. He couldn't possibly have any idea of his twin's personality because he or she, being merely an embryo, had not yet formed one; therefore he could not know; he could only feel the absence.

'All along here,' he said, as he drew his hand the long length of his body: all his life, he'd had this sense of something missing.

I don't know - he didn't tell me and I didn't ask - whether Bill missed me when our relationship gave up the ghost and died as Jupiter gave way to Neptune. Not that it ended as such. Rather it simply petered-out, getting thinner and thinner each day during the summer I began my search for Dorothy; rather a difficult period as I recall.

Yes, yes, I know, I should have seen it coming, but I didn't. Well, that's not strictly true, I got a whiff of it, let's say, but I didn't look very carefully. I saw the, 'big guns,' Saturn and Mars approaching my Sun and Midheaven and thought, maybe I'll get a promotion at school. I saw Neptune and wondered if I might start painting again. I saw Uranus poised to strike my Descendant and thought, maybe Bill will take up Astrology; that'd be a shock. Yes, well, it would have been. It would have been one hell of an almighty shock, but that's not what happened.

What happened was this: - my mother suffered a massive stroke; my skin broke out in eczema; and Bill became depressed.

At first, I didn't pay much attention to Bill's unhappiness. He'd been depressed before, I reasoned: this was his Philosopher's Melancholy. Sooner or later, he would resurface and things would carry on as before. Meanwhile, I carried on as before: teaching, shopping, nursing my mother, casting my charts and ignoring all the signs that our relationship was ending. And yet, because there wasn't an ending, I kept it in mind, imagining, what, that it had just gone off on holiday somewhere - which was how I had coped when my father died. I had coped then with images: images of unpacked suitcases; buckets and spades propped up in the hall; Cheap Day Returns which would never expire. Likewise with Bill, with our relationship: a tartan blanket stretched across an empty expanse of sand. Ah, well, the weather hadn't been too good lately: sooner or later, he would emerge and we would all just carry on as before. But as the weeks turned into months with still no contact, I began to worry. He wasn't answering his telephone. I hadn't seen him out and about. Friends had nothing to report. At last, I consulted my Ephemeris.

Sure enough, he had some difficult transits going on. And as I pondered the symbolism, my imagination took a turn for the worse. For Saturn rules endings and Neptune rules the waves. It wasn't beyond the bounds of possibility that like his stoical great grandfather, the captain of a North Sea trawler, Bill was choosing to go down with his ship.

Friends sought to reassure me: Bill's a survivor, they said. Fellow astrologers advised me to look at my own chart and desist from worrying his. And they were right, for I too was labouring under a similar alignment: - but worrying unduly, as it turned out. In my anxiety, I had overlooked the most obvious manifestation of a Neptune Venus transit: the urge to lose oneself in another, to transcend mundane reality in a dream of love. He wasn't going down with his ship; he was coming out of his house with a tall and slender blonde dressed from top to tail in black.

'It *was* a woman,' Eleanor insisted as I pushed my foot down on the accelerator. 'It wasn't one of his students needing comfort. It was another woman. Honestly, Mum, when are you going to wake up?'

Yes, well: good question. If only I had noted the time, I could have cast the Horary Chart: 'My Neptunian Mother When Will She Wake Up?' But this wasn't a Horary Moment. I didn't look at my watch. I didn't clock the time on the dashboard. Nor did I check the positions of the planets when I got home. I did, however, pay a lot more attention a few days later, when I awoke from a powerful dream.

I had fallen asleep on the sofa and dreamed that Bill was in an underground tunnel gathering snails while I splashed around in the shallow water behind him, trying to attract his attention. This failing, I followed him out of the tunnel along a familiar street, then into the staircase hall of a large Edwardian house. Here, he was warmly-greeted by the same young blonde, now wearing gold not black, who took him into her arms beneath an enormous crystal chandelier.

Any minute now, I thought, that chandelier's going to come crashing down and we'll all be shot to pieces. So I took myself out of that scenario, landing in Bill's study instead. Here, I unearthed a horoscope (not one of mine) which had the glyph for the sign of Taurus stamped on the front. It all but obliterated the chart. What could this mean, I wondered; could this be Bill's Ascendant? But before I could answer that question, I woke up. And, when I woke, I knew that if I left the house at that very moment then I would see him.

Now, this isn't like me. Without stopping to inform Eleanor; without checking on my mother, dowsing the ashtray or pulling out the plugs - and pausing only to note the time - I sped through my house and into my car, and drove off in the direction of the street I had seen in my dream. Sure enough, there he was. He was just about to turn the corner when I saw him and flagged him down.

Close up, I barely recognised him; he looked so different. Oh, he had always been handsome: tall and dark with deep brown eyes and cheekbones to cut your teeth on; but when we were together, there had been a greyness about him which seemed to blur his edges. Now he looked sharper, cleaner; animated. His hair was cut short; his clothes were pressed; his fingernails were trimmed: he was in love.

Her name was Maddy, he told me, short for Madeleine; and yes, I was right: he <u>was</u> on his way to see her; and, yes, she <u>did</u> live in one of the large Edwardian houses nearby. Furthermore, he was very interested to hear of my dream because they had quarrelled that very afternoon, and he took this as a sign that they would surely be reconciled.

'Funny things keep happening to me at the moment,' he said, 'the Cosmos keeps giving me presents.'

I believe my mouth may have fallen open at this point: could this be the same rational, sceptical man, or was I still asleep? I looked down at my feet. No, I wasn't still asleep, I was standing on the pavement in a pile of old chip wrappings.

'Are you all right?' Bill asked.

'Oh, yes, I'm fine.' This could well have been true: I was still marvelling at my dream.

Bill's tone, however, had darkened. 'Hmm, but what are you really doing here, I wonder?'

'It's exactly as I said,' I replied. 'I had this dream, and when I woke, I knew that if I left the house at once then I would see you. And here I am. And here you are. Well, don't you think that's extraordinary? Aren't you surprised?'

'I'm not surprised, no, that you're more interested in your dream than in reality.'

'Oh, but it's the same reality - sort of. Oh, well, never mind, I had the dream so now I know.'

'Know what?'

'That you've met someone!'

'You knew that already.'

'No, I didn't.'

'Yes, you did. You saw me, or Eleanor did. You drove past in your car and Eleanor saw me. And gave me a filthy look, I might add.'

'Did she? Oh, I'm sorry. But, the thing is, I didn't realise. I mean, I hadn't taken it in. But now I have, so that's all right.'

'You're sure about that, are you?'

'Yes, I think so – although I was wondering when you met her.'

'Ah, of course,' he brightened again. 'You'll want to do the chart.'

'No, I'm not sure that I do, Bill. In fact, I think I probably don't. No, I was wondering whether you met her while you and I –'

He moved in quickly to reassure me: 'No, no, not at all. It's not what you're thinking at all. We met a fortnight ago - give or take a day or two on either side. Well, I'm sorry I can't be more specific, but you know how it is.'

I wasn't sure that I did know how 'it' was. It all sounded very strange to me. But I listened very carefully to his account of how it was for him.

She was a Godsend: his Redemption; and he had never felt this way before. For she was everything he had ever dreamed of: bold, spirited and fiercely, ruthlessly honest. Better still, they had so much in common: they enjoyed the same tastes; shared the same beliefs and came from the same northern neck of the woods. They even shared - now, this would interest me - the same birthday: different years, of course, but the same glorious February day. So, what did I make of that?

Not much, I thought, but decided against offering the benefit of an astrological consultation at this point. By now, I was beginning to feel upset.

'Sounds like you've met your twin,' I said at last.

'Oh, I have. I have.'

I swallowed hard as I watched him draw his hand all the way down his body.

'All along here,' he said, beaming. 'All along here, it finally fits.'

'Well, perhaps we can say goodbye now, Bill. We should have done so earlier, really.'

But his expression darkened again as he pondered the word, 'goodbye,' rolling it around on his tongue. 'No, I think not.' As if I had been trying to palm him off with faulty goods. 'I will never say goodbye to you, Gwendolen. I still love you and I always will. Nothing changes that. You know me, I never let go.'

And with that; with a business-as-usual wave; he turned on his heels and resumed his journey.

'Well, I don't know, Dorothy,' I said when I got to the churchyard. 'It's a fine-sounding word, isn't it, Love, but what does it really mean?' And I stooped to run my fingers along the inscription. 'What do these words you've got here, which sound so beautiful, really mean? I wonder.

Forgive me, Dorothy, but could it have been guilt, or even pity? You were dying. Peter felt sorry for you. Maybe he let you down in some way? He may even have betrayed you. So, it could have been for himself and not for you that he cast this inscription. Out of guilt, or pity, not love. He may never have loved you at all.

I'm sorry, Dorothy, and I hope you'll forgive me if I've got it all wrong, but I really need to know the truth. So, what do you think? Would it be all right with you if I tried to find out?'

I had been crouching beside the grave, supporting myself with one hand on the headstone. Now, as I moved to get up, I toppled over. The sun had long gone down but the earth was still warm. I scooped up a fistful and held it tightly. It felt good. It felt like making a pact.

PLUTO

Looking through my Ephemeris now, I can see why I began my search for Dorothy during August 1999, though I wasn't exactly monitoring it astrologically at the time. Believe it or not, I rarely consult the Heavens before I act, partly because I forget, but mainly because I prefer to observe events through Astrology as they unfold. And I now observe that Pluto, Lord of the Underworld, was transiting a key point in my Conception Chart when I began my search. Yes, thanks to my mercurial mother's meticulous record keeping, I have the precise date, location and prevailing weather conditions of my conception: July 11th 1956, Blackpool; at 11:56. p.m.: 'Hot and Misty'. She felt a, 'ping,' apparently.

Ping, and all the lights went on in Blackpool. Ping, and I announced my intention to incarnate. Ping, and my mother reached for her Good Housekeeping diary: - and all on the anniversary of Dorothy Browning's death.

Had I been aware of this coincidence, I wondered, when I first found Dorothy's grave? It didn't strike me as likely. I wasn't remotely interested in the laborious contents of my mother's Good Housekeeping diaries before I took up Astrology; and one thing is for sure, I must have found Dorothy's grave before I discovered Astrology – otherwise I'd have dashed straight back home from the churchyard and done the chart.

I looked up at my mother, enthroned on her Parker Knoll chair. 'Not much of an entrance, was it?'

'I don't know what you mean.'

'I felt an explosion when I conceived Eleanor. And I had a dream the same night of a baby girl; *and* the initial letter, E, all lit up.'

'Oh yes, well, you always have to do better than anyone else – or the opposite. If I'd said mine was an explosion, you'd have said yours was a ping.'

'No, I wouldn't.'

'Yes, you would. I should have called you Mary - Mary, Mary, quite contrary - but even if I had done, it would still have been a ping I felt. I know my own body.'

'Yes, but you might not have been ovulating.'

'Of course I was, or I wouldn't have caught for you would I!'

'Well then, couldn't it have been some kind of muscular spasm?'

'No. It wasn't a spasm, it was you. I ought to know, I was there and you weren't. Not for another nine months. And even then you were late. One of these days, you'll arrive somewhere on time. I just hope I live to see it.'

I arrived on the 19th of April 1957 during the lunch hour, in a nursing home run by Anglican nuns. Why my mother, a lapsed Welsh Baptist; and father, an agnostic with Zen sympathies, chose such a venue, I can't imagine, especially since my father thoroughly disliked organised religion and used to delight in sending Mormons and Jehovah's Witnesses round to the Roman Catholic Archbishop of Wales who lived next door.

'Now, I know someone,' he would say, 'who would be very interested in your ideas.'

Meanwhile, my mother surely regretted her choice of Anglican nuns as midwives because when it came to the crunch - as she so delicately put it - they were nowhere to be seen. It was Good Friday so they were all down in the chapel praying which meant she had to deliver me herself. Knowing her, this wouldn't have been too difficult. She'd have approached it in her, 'Dig for Victory,' manner then given the nuns a very bad time for putting spiritual concerns above practical realities. Perhaps that's unfair; but it's certainly how she approached me: -

'I was hoping you'd find something more useful to do with my diaries instead of rooting around in them for your Astrology,' she complained, 'I told you, I want you to donate them to the Imperial War Museum.'

'I don't see why I should, they're a family heirloom. Besides, what would the Imperial War Museum want with your Good Housekeeping diaries?'

'I didn't mean them, I meant my War diaries. Oh, but you've never been interested in my war. It was always your father's war with you. Well, mine lasted longer than his.'

'Yes, that was hardly his fault, Mum. Anyway, I am interested in your war. It's just that - at the moment - I'm more interested in your Good Housekeeping diaries. Tut, if only I'd told you about Dorothy's grave at the time I found it - because then you'd have written it down, wouldn't you, saving me a lot of bother.'

'I would have,' she replied, looking very pleased with herself. 'Well, perhaps you'll see the value of it now and start becoming organised. You would never listen to me but you might just take the hint from Dorothy Browning.'

I smiled, watching her drift off to sleep. By now, for all her pragmatism, she too had become intrigued by Dorothy's inscription, keeping a copy inside her wallet along with the last letter she received from her Great Love, Jimmy, the officer she'd met while nursing in North Africa during the War. Every so often, she would take out this missive and hold it up to the light, as if trying to read something different into those final words: Not Goodbye, <u>Please</u>. She would then bring out Dorothy's inscription and gaze at it thoughtfully, as if it contained the antidote. Not that she believed in Life after Death. Her only surviving brother, Glenville, however, did. And, as if to make his point, he expired within days of receiving his copy of the inscription, having taken it as a sign, (or so he told my mother in his thank you letter) that he would surely be reunited with <u>his</u> Dorothy: his wife who had died young.

After this, although she would never condone it, my mother became less hostile to my Astrology; although she still got considerable mileage out of my inability to tell her whether she was a Leo or a Virgo.

In vain I would protest: 'You're on the cusp.'

'Oh, yes, you'll have worked it out, I suppose, by the time I'm gone. And then I can look forward to a horoscope on my headstone.'

It's hard for me to write about my mother as another anniversary looms, yet I know that if she hadn't decided to return to Wales that summer, and enter a nursing home, I wouldn't have made much progress with my search for Dorothy: I wouldn't have had the time or the energy. If it hadn't been for Bill too; if he hadn't met his twin in the same fateful period, I very much doubt that my Pluto transit would have found me, as a member of my Sixth-form once so aptly put it: 'Stalking the dead again, Miss.' This time, in Oxford Central Library.

I began my search on a particularly heavy and humid day, as I recall. Eleanor had gone swimming with friends from Ballet so I had the whole day to myself. Arriving early in the morning, I made straight for the second floor. Happily, I already knew my way around the system, having spent much of the previous summer immured in there researching my Astrological Family Tree. As well as dates, there are Sun signs, Moon signs, aspects and elements.

On my father's side, there was an emphasis on Fixed Earth (coal-miners and allotment enthusiasts) as well as Fixed Air (armchair philosophers). On my mother's side, there was more variety; with many a sea-faring uncle born under dreamy, variable Pisces; and an equal abundance of home-loving aunts clocking in under the Moon's sign of Cancer. The women who'd left home, like my mother, tended to have Leo and Virgo strongly emphasised as, no doubt, they went off to direct operations and be of useful service in the world.

Now, where would Dorothy fit into this picture, I wondered, if at all? More importantly, what kind of woman could inspire such an inscription? I would need her date of birth in order to find out; and in order to get that, I would have to locate the record of her death. This would reveal her age at death, as well as her marital status, and I could work backwards from there. So, heading straight for the Index for 1947, I found the slide I wanted and slipped it into the Microfiche Reader, winding it forwards and backwards again, and again – and again. She wasn't there. A mere handful of Brownings had died during the summer of 1947, and not one of them called Dorothy.

'This can't be right, this just cannot be right. A death's gone missing,' I exclaimed, provoking a sharply-hissed, 'Be quiet,' from the woman sitting beside me. Given her bird-of-prey features, blue-black hair; and, very likely, Scorpio Ascendant, I decided against retaliating, but headed off, as she pointedly indicated, towards the main desk. Here, the librarian, a man of about my age with generous features, pale grey eyes and a soft brown beard, appeared a distinctly less formidable prospect.

'Excuse me,' I said, passing him Dorothy's inscription. 'I'm sorry to bother you but I appear to have lost this person and I was wondering if you could help. I can't find the record of her death in the Index. Could it have happened that her death wasn't registered?'

Frowning, he stroked his beard, 'I wouldn't have thought so. Well, how very unusual.'

'It doesn't happen then?'

'No, I meant the inscription. It's very unusual, isn't it? Remarkable, really. I wonder what it means.'

'So do I,' I replied. 'But if I can't get hold of the record, I'm not going to be able to find out. I've got nothing else to go on, you see.'

'She isn't a family member then?'

'No, more of a family friend.' I then gave him an account of my experience in the churchyard the day I discovered her grave. At last I had found a sympathetic audience.

'It's lovely,' he said, nodding thoughtfully. 'The whole thing's intriguing. And you say you've checked the Index and she isn't there?'

'That's right, no sign of her.'

'Well, now, I wonder - and this is just a thought - it could be the wrong name on her headstone. Her death will have been registered, I'm sure, under her legal name; but it isn't a legal requirement to put the correct name on the headstone.'

'What? Oh, no, surely it must be?'

'I'm afraid not. It's only a legal requirement to register a death. You can put what you like on the headstone.'

'Oh, but that's appalling,' I protested, 'I mean, that's just not on, is it. I mean, my name's Gwendolen Gaskell, but this means that when I die, any old Tom, Dick or Harry could come along and write, 'Here lies Jemima Puddleduck,' on my headstone and I wouldn't be able to do the first thing about it!'

'Er, no, probably not. But why would anyone in your family wish to do that?'

'Why indeed! Why would Peter want to put the wrong name on Dorothy's headstone? It's beyond me.'

Thankfully, it wasn't beyond the librarian.

'Well now,' he said kindly, 'let's suppose they weren't married but were living together. When did she die, forty-seven? I should think it would still have been something of a stigma, wouldn't you say so, living in sin. She could well have called herself Browning to make it more acceptable. Or, she may have preferred his surname to her own. People do that quite often.'

'Well, I wish they wouldn't,' I replied irritably. 'Because names are important. Your whole destiny's in your name. Why else would we bother with, you know: 'Their Name Liveth Forever More?''

'Ah, yes. Quite. But people still do that kind of thing.'

I nodded. 'You're right, aren't you, which means I'm stumped because there's no way I'm going to be able to track down Peter with nothing whatsoever to go on. I don't know whether he lived in Oxford. I don't know whether he's dead or alive. In fact, I've got no impression of him at all.'

'It doesn't sound too hopeful, I agree. But, you know, you mustn't give up. Again, this is just a thought, but there's a chance they put the correct name in the burial register. You said you tried the Church?'

'Yes, the vicar said it wasn't there. Oh, but this was ages ago.'

At this, he brightened. 'In that case, you could be in luck, and it'll have been deposited in the County Archives. They don't always remember, but parish priests are supposed to deposit the registers after fifty years.'

Then, taking a last look at the inscription, which, by now, he must have known off by heart, he gave me a wistful smile and added, 'It's quite a mystery, isn't it. I do hope you find her. She must have been quite an inspiration in her day.'

'She still is,' I replied, and he wished me luck as I left.

As luck would have it, however, the Archives were closed when I arrived. Undeterred, I returned the next day, clutching a brand new notebook. Again, I was on familiar territory: that is, the Archives felt familiar, reminding me of the cluttered stacks and gloomy reading rooms I had visited as a none-too-diligent student of History some twenty years before. Indeed, the assembled readers could well have been the same individuals. Still dressed for silence, in corduroy trousers and soft cardigans, they padded round in shoes with rubber soles, and, in one case, carpet slippers. Only the archivist looked out of place in this dismal basement. Wearing a bright blue boiler suit, scarlet hair band, and quilted waistcoat; she looked as though she would have been far happier working in the Great Outdoors, especially since her whole demeanour suggested someone who invariably made the best of bad weather.

'Oh, not to worry, I'm sure we can crack this one,' she said breezily, upon hearing my account of missing deaths and careless clergymen – at which point I received the distinct impression that she was a reincarnated W.A.A.F.

'Now, let's have a look-see, shall we,' she added, opening the Catalogue whereupon she broke into a delighted smile. 'Ah, yes, we do have it. It was deposited in '97. Well, that solves your problem.'

'Thank God for that,' I said to myself as I watched her disappear into the Stacks; and, before long, I was relaxing back into a chair and planning my next moves. I would probably have to wait a week or so for the Death Certificate to arrive. Meanwhile, equipped, as I shortly would be, with Dorothy's correct surname, I could look in the Somerset House Index of Wills to see whether she had left anything to Peter. I could then enjoy a leisurely browse through the Newspaper Archive. With any luck a school or wedding photograph would appear: -

With any luck the parish register would appear.

What was she doing in there? Why was she taking so long? Had she been distracted by one of the assembled readers, or stopped for a chat with a colleague?

Apparently not.

She had been checking, she explained. She had checked and doubled checked. She had also asked her colleague to assist her. It wasn't there.

'I'm very sorry,' she added, 'I just don't know what to say to you. Believe me, this has never happened before. According to the Log, we've definitely got it. Only, it isn't where it should be, or anywhere else.'

I took a deep breath, 'Is it possible – could someone have borrowed it?'

'Oh, no, this isn't a library!'

'Well then, could someone have borrowed it unofficially? I expect you get all sorts of people coming in here off the street.'

'We do. But that certainly won't have happened.'

But I was following my own train of thought: 'Someone with a fetish for mouldering documents, perhaps - or a grudge against the Church of England. It is just possible, isn't it, that it's been stolen!'

'No.' she replied. 'It is not. We are very careful about security in here. If you remember, you had to leave your bag at the door.'

Clearly, I had upset her, so I apologised: 'I'm a bit over-wrought at the moment. Things aren't too brilliant on the Home Front. I'm very sorry if I was rude.'

'Oh, that's all right,' she said, and, upon sitting down, adopted a more confidential tone, intended to reassure me, I supposed, although it had the opposite effect.

'Actually, you weren't too far off in what you implied. We do get all sorts of odd bods coming in here off the street. You wouldn't believe some of the things they do with the registers: ripping out pages, scribbling in the margins; and leaving all sorts of things inside, from book marks to bus tickets and even more personal items.'

'Personal items?'

'Oh, yes,' she said, raising her eyebrows and giving me a knowing look: 'And a lot of what they write, I'm afraid some of it's quite obscene. But, you know, it really wouldn't be possible to make off with an entire parish register. You can imagine how heavy they are, and how cumbersome. It's not the sort of thing you could easily slip under your coat. No, I can promise you it hasn't been stolen.'

I nodded before venturing another possibility, 'I don't suppose the vicar could have changed his mind and come back for it later?' But before she could respond, I anticipated her reply: 'No, you'd have logged it out again, wouldn't you.'

'Yes. Believe me, we really are meticulous in here.'

'Thought so,' I said flatly.

And we gazed at each other, defeated.

'If you do manage to track it down,' she asked, as I reached for my jacket, 'I'd be very grateful if you could let me know, I'm quite upset about it myself.'

'Yes, of course,' I nodded, although I didn't hold out a lot of hope.

By now, I was feeling thoroughly dispirited, exhausted and close to tears, so I stopped at a kiosk on Cornmarket Street and bought several muffins which I ate while pondering the fate of the parish register on my bus journey home.

The vicar had deposited it in 1997. Now, two years later, it was missing. It wasn't beyond the bounds of possibility that it had been stolen, but by whom? Who, in their right mind, would want to steal a parish register? No, despite her insistence to the contrary, it seemed more likely that someone in the Archivists' Office had slipped up. The vicar could well have returned and withdrawn it without signing it out, but why? Why would the vicar want it back? And why tell me it wasn't in the church? Unless? Unless it contained some dire and desperate secret he wished to conceal. Had the vicar, like one of the archivist's 'odd bods' been scribbling in the text?

Once again, my imagination took a turn for the worse as it conjured up an image of the vicar - a cross between Aleister Crowley and a Second World War spiv - using a hollowed-out parish register, inscribed with all manner of reptilian runes, as his hidey-hole for casino winnings, lottery tickets and crack cocaine. Either that, or it was currently plugging a gap in the floor boards, propping up his dining table, or serving as an improvised press for his ancient aunt Euphemia's collection of wild flowers. Well, what else would you do with a parish register? Try as I might, I couldn't think of an alternative. Nor could I imagine the means by which it might be brought to light. Indeed, I had about as much chance of meeting Dorothy Browning herself, alive and well and working in the esoteric bookshop as of exacting a confession from the vicar. He may have lost it. He may never have had it. It could even have been stolen from the Rectory. No, I had to face the fact that it was probably gone for good, and that my search for Dorothy had ended before it had even begun.

'Things couldn't be worse,' I muttered, descending from my bus at the wrong stop. Oh, but yes they could. Just outside Tesco, I bumped into Bill. And he, of course, was looking the very picture of health and happiness; not to mention fifteen years younger in a dark red velvet jacket, crisply laundered shirt and brand new jet black trousers. All he needed was a carnation in his buttonhole to look the perfect groom. Could I commit murder, I wondered, in the foyer of a major supermarket, and get away with it? Probably not. Besides, what would I do – stuff him with muffin wrappings?

'Are you all right?' he asked amiably. 'Only you don't look too good.'

'Thank you, Bill, I'm fine.'

'Come on. Something's wrong. I know you. What's up?'

So, I told him as we walked along. Because I didn't want to talk about, 'us,' or, worse, hear about, 'them,' I told him about my abortive search for Dorothy.

'Well, now,' he said, as I ground to a halt, 'that is interesting. I wonder who it is that's buried there, if not her - not that it matters, of course.'

'What do you mean, not that it matters? Of course it matters. Anyway, she is buried there. I ought to know, I found her myself.'

'It shouldn't make any difference who is buried there, since, as you tell me, this is a spiritual quest.'

'It makes a difference to me,' I snapped. 'Without her correct surname, I can't find the record of her death. And without her Death Certificate, I won't be able to find out when out when she was born - which means I won't be able to do her Horoscope.'

'Ah, madness, madness,' he exclaimed, clapping his hands over his ears and skipping a few paces ahead.

'I want to compare Dorothy's chart with mine,' I said, running to catch up with him. 'I want to see whether there's any connection between us. If there isn't, I'll leave well alone, but if there is, I'll pursue it. It might explain things. It might explain why I'm drawn there, why I had that strange experience in the churchyard the day I found her grave.'

'Ah, but she has chosen not to reveal herself to you. She prefers to remain anonymous. Her secret died with her. And that's how it should be.'

'You can't know that.'

'I can and I do. And you need to hear this. If you could only accept things the way they are, you'd be so much happier - because you're not happy, are you? For you, there always has to be something else. Look, you found this grave. Dorothy Browning's? Maybe. It doesn't matter who's buried there because what you experienced was real. And it was real because it came from you. It was a gift; if you like, a present from self to self. But what do you do with it? You push it away 'up there' because you can't accept presents. But, of course, it turns out that what you thought was there isn't there after all. Dorothy Browning isn't buried there. I'd say there was a message in that!'

I turned my head away.

'You've still got it,' he said, softening, 'what you found there. You haven't lost anything.'

Oh, but I had. And what's more, I could now feel it. So, I quickly took my leave of him and darted into the nearest shop. I didn't want any food. I didn't want any flowers. I didn't want him to see me cry. My only consolation was that I had maintained my dignity throughout.

'Bill says you don't exist,' I told Dorothy when I got to the churchyard.

'It's a bit much, isn't it, all these people denying your existence. First the vicar. Now Bill. And, maybe, even Peter.'

And I moved to scrape my boot along the headstone, dislodging a cluster of snails.

'But I believe in you,' I whispered as it began to rain.

That night I slept badly. Various faces, emerging in the darkness, disturbed my sleep: Bill's face; his twin's; my mother's. A man I didn't recognise; his forehead obscured under the brim of a dark brown felt hat. Like Bill around the mouth, but not Bill. Older, sadder, thinner: defeated – my father?

No, here was my beautiful father: high, proud forehead; wide cheekbones; clear brown eyes gazing wistfully ahead. My father in his red beret: circa 1944. My father before the bullet. Before the bullet which shattered his face, and dreams of love; sending him into the lonely dark forever.

Blinking, I opened my eyes very wide and called out his name but there was no reply. Leaving my bed, I went to the window and drew back the curtains but he wasn't in the garden either.

Bill's words had gone very deep. They now resurfaced as I lay on the bed and wept. Supposing Bill was right? Supposing he had been right all along, and I had imagined everything out of the ordinary which had ever happened to me. If he <u>was</u> right, and I had merely invented them; then they were nothing. They were all dead and gone, and I was absolutely, fundamentally alone. Worse, I had wilfully brought this about in my desire for Something Other. In my desire for another reality, I had sacrificed the one I already had; for hadn't Bill always said I was never there for him; never fully available? So, now, I had lost him too. And as these thoughts struck home, I felt myself falling into a very dark place. I did not go there willingly. I fought bodily against it, clinging on in the pit of my stomach. But it was no good. In the end, I had to go there.

I can't remember how long I remained there, although I do remember calling out to Eleanor that I was sick with 'flu' and that she must telephone friends for help. The help duly arrived. I could vaguely hear it busying itself downstairs while I lay on the bed; not thinking; nor praying, merely occupying space and feeling nothing.

At first, it felt hateful, this nothing: thick, black, dense, oppressive; but after a while, I got used to it. So, that was that then: nothing. And, after a while, I felt okay. I felt the same inside, and the same way about everyone else. So that was that then. Back to life. I got up; went to the bathroom, washed my hair and brushed my teeth. I went downstairs, took Eleanor shopping; visited my mother, and returned to school. And then, one day towards the end of September, I took a bunch of flowers down to Dorothy's grave. I didn't feel much like talking. I hadn't got any news. I just tidied things up a bit then returned along the pathway behind the church.

A side door in the vestry was open, and, as I approached, a priest came out. He popped out, scratched his head, and popped back in again. By then, it was beginning to dawn on me, so I waited.

'Excuse me,' I said, when he reappeared. 'Are you the vicar?'

'I am. May I help you?'

'Are you the new vicar - or are you just visiting?'

'I am the new vicar, yes. Is there something I can help you with?'

'There is,' I replied. 'Though it might strike you as rather odd.'

If it did strike him as odd, he showed no sign, but replied in a business-like manner. One of his first tasks, upon taking over the incumbency, had been to sort the registers out. He could therefore assure me that they were all present and correct. Meanwhile, he was rather busy, preparing for Evensong, but if I were to return in an hour or so, I could browse at my leisure.

We returned, self and Eleanor, at 5.30 p.m. I had asked her to accompany me, thinking she might like to participate in this historic event; and, on reflection, I can only say that it's a good job she agreed - because it was Eleanor who found Dorothy. As usual, I had been looking in the wrong place. I'd been looking in the register of burials for 1947. But Dorothy Margaret Browning had died the previous year.

'Here she is,' she announced, 'July 11th 1946. Right body, wrong date.'

So, we had solved our mystery; yet we were never able to discover how the parish register, deposited in the County Archive two years before had made its way back to the Church.

'Not young then,' said Eleanor, taking my arm as we walked back down the aisle.

'Oh, I wouldn't call forty-five old.'

'No, you wouldn't, would you. Still, never mind, you're not there yet.'

'Not quite.'

'Funny her having the same middle name as you though.'

'I don't know,' I replied. 'It's a common enough name, Margaret. Anyway, it's your middle name as well.'

'I know, don't remind me. I don't know why you had to give me such old-fashioned names.'

'You're an old-fashioned girl.'

'No, I'm not. Come on, Mum. What is it?'

'Hmm?'

'Well, we've found her but you don't seem very pleased.'

'Oh, I expect I'm just tired. After all, it has been rather a long haul. I should think it's just a bit of an anti-climax. But, well done sweetheart. You did really well. Of course I'm pleased.'

'You'll be able to send off for her Death Certificate now; that should cheer you up.' I laughed, but somehow I didn't think it would. I had the feeling I already knew how she had died.

Later that same evening, I drew up the chart for this moment of discovery. Uranus has just risen with the fateful South Node of the Moon while Pluto culminates at the Midheaven: - something buried comes to light.

SATURN

This is going to be a very short chapter because Saturn limits things. He also rules everything cold, hard, bitter, barren and bleak. Oh, but I should look on the bright side, for it occurs to me now that anyone who perseveres with this chapter will surely be constellating true grit: monks, martyrs, miners and monogamists - read on.

The first thing I did upon opening Dorothy's Death Certificate was to draw up the chart for the moment I had received it. In this kind of chart, the person who acts or enquires is symbolised by the planet ruling the Sign on the Ascendant; the other party by the planet ruling the Sign on the Descendant, the opposite point. So, here I am, Saturn, ruler of the Capricorn Ascendant; and here is Dorothy, the Moon ruling Cancer on the opposite point. And here we are together. We are in this plot together: Saturn conjoining the Moon at the Nadir, the point of the grave.

Am I about to peg it – was my first thought. Had she come to warn me? Was <u>this</u> the reason I had found Dorothy's grave – because I needed a Cosmic Medical Reminder? In fact, should I not get myself off to the Health Centre right now before it closed? Yet somehow I couldn't quite envisage the following scenario (though I'm sure I did my best).

'Hello, Dr Robbins.'

'Good afternoon, Gwendolen. Now, what can we do for you today? I'm afraid we haven't heard from Dermatology yet. How are those hands and feet?'

'Oh, not too bad, you know, Doctor. Still hobbling. But it's not my skin I've come to see you about today. I was wondering whether you could arrange for me to see a gynaecologist.'

'Oh yes? Any particular reason?'

'I have just discovered that the woman whose grave I've been tending for many a long and lonely year died of the same thing as me.'

'Really? Do you know, I don't recall certifying you as dead? Perhaps it was one of my colleagues. We're very busy at the moment, of course, and struggling to keep on top of the paper work.'

'Oh, dear, I'm sorry to hear that. I blame government initiatives, don't you? We get exactly same thing to contend with at school so I can sympathise. And, believe me, I'm reluctant to add to your workload: it's just that I was wondering: could you arrange for me to have a scan, just in case?'

Hmm, no, I couldn't quite see that request going down too well with the hard-pressed clinicians at the Health Centre. They already had enough difficulty treating my eczema without having to work their magic on posthumous complaints. Best not, I thought. Best deal with it myself.

Closing my eyes, I slipped my hand inside my skirt and moved it across my abdomen, tracing the jagged outline of the old scar. No, I couldn't feel anything, no unusual lumps or swelling. Nothing to worry about there. So, why was I sweating, and feeling increasingly nauseous? After a cup of camomile tea and a walk in the garden did nothing to calm me down, I telephoned my astrological pen friend, Richard.

'I'm sure you're fine,' he said. 'It's an odd thing but I wouldn't dwell on it. She died, you didn't. Leave it at that.'

'But, Richard, I nearly died. And you know I've always been terrified of anaesthetics. I was four hours on the slab.'

'Never mind, you're not on it now. You lost your ovary; she lost her life. You survived, that's the point.'

'Yes, but I've always had this fear that they were lying to protect me when they said it was benign – because they couldn't bear to tell a young girl the truth and crush her hope of life.'

'No,' he said firmly. 'That's the kind of thing you do. I'm quite sure this wasn't the case. By all means, go and get yourself checked out if you think it'll help, but I'm sure you'll find nothing wrong. Now, if I were you, I'd go out and get some fresh air. Better still, do something creative. How about doing some painting?'

'I can't,' I wailed, 'my hands.'

'Oh, yes, of course. Well, never mind. Put some gloves on, and go and do some gardening. You love your garden, I know. Or go out and do something you'll enjoy with Eleanor. Hmm, now, that's thought. Did Dorothy have any children?'

'I don't know. My feeling is she didn't. But why? Do you think that's relevant?'

'It was just a thought. But then you've got Eleanor. You had Eleanor against the odds, that's the point; so don't dwell on it, Gwen. Leave it in the past where it belongs - and do the same with Bill.'

I sighed. 'That's easier said than done.'

'Even so, you must do it.'

'Did I tell you they're getting married?'

'You did, the last time we spoke.'

'He asked Eleanor to be their bridesmaid.'

'So you told me. And she refused, didn't she, which is all that need concern you. Put it behind you now, and leave them to it. It's not your karma. This is about your future, not your past. You'll be all right, I'm sure.'

'I, I don't really think it's coming back.'

'Neither do I.'

'I just needed to tell someone, you know, what I feared - get it out in the open.'

'I know.'

'So, thank you very much.'

'Put it behind you, now, Gwen. Go out and get some fresh air in the sunlight. That's the best antidote to Saturn.'

Well, that was very good advice, I thought, as I replaced the receiver; and I had every intention of following it; but then just as I went to put the certificate away, something else caught my eye.

Dorothy had been married; but not to Peter!

She had been the wife of Wilfrid, George, Brunet, Browning, to be precise.

So, where was the Peter, I wondered, on July 11th 1946? Not to mention the next day, when Wilfrid Browning registered Dorothy's death? Come to think of it, where was Wilfrid when Peter cast the inscription? Perhaps, by then, he, too, was dead; for surely had her husband been alive, he would not have allowed another man to cast such a personal inscription? Unless Peter was their son - an unusually poetic son.

The plot thickened. The plot thickened darkly as my mood plummeted further: for, if Wilfrid had been Dorothy's husband, and Peter had been her lover, then she had not been the Innocent I had imagined, which meant that for all these years I had been loyally tending the grave of a woman who had failed to keep her vows. Even worse, I'd involved my mother in it. And it struck me, there and then, that the Universe was enjoying a very black joke at our expense. How Bill would have enjoyed the irony. I could almost see him nodding sagely then breaking into a sardonic smile because if there was one thing, apart from religion, that he and I could be guaranteed to argue about, it was morality. He had never believed my protestations that I was the Faithful Type.

'The lady doth protest too much, methinks,' I recalled him saying. 'And indeed, your choice of language makes me suspicious; your use of the word 'attachment,' in particular. This suggests something extra, that your beliefs have been added on from outside. You are 'attached' to the idea of Fidelity. Now, where might that idea have come from?'

'It comes from me. I know what I'm like. When I love someone, I'm not interested in sleeping with anyone else. I am the Faithful Type, a One Man Woman.'

'Oh yes? And how many lovers was it at the last count?'

'Nowhere near as many as you. And none of mine were married. And I have never been married.'

'No, and it's precisely because you have never married that you cannot judge. Nor should you, of course. But I must say, I do find it interesting that you have never married. After all, it's not as though you've never been asked - and many times by your own account. Could it be that you're reluctant to put your principles to the test; that you're unwilling to take the risk, because then you might discover what you're really like, and what you do believe for yourself, and you might be surprised.'

I hadn't thought so. I hadn't thought so then and saw no reason to change my mind now on the off chance that Dorothy had a lover. I might still desire Bill, but I could no more sleep with him now that he was engaged to be married than take off in an aeroplane or go to bed without pulling out the plugs.

Sure?

Quite sure.

Not even to outshine her?

No. Though, of course, I could - if I wanted to. She hadn't looked that hot to me. Quite the opposite in fact. She'd looked cold and raw-boned, dressed from top to tail in black. Of course I could, if I wanted to. I might even enjoy it. Yes, just for the hell of it. Oh, I knew him all right; I knew his Achilles Heel. Ah, but it wouldn't be worth it. It wouldn't be worth all the guilt and agonising and self-recrimination afterwards (on his part not mine). No, I couldn't be bothered. Not even to outshine her. I had better things to do with my time.

But who was I kidding? Of course he wouldn't be back, not now he'd met his twin. The truth was; he no longer needed me. I was redundant. I had been rendered invisible; driven underground. No wonder I identified with a dead woman.

Dead: - but not quite. She still had something to say. I looked at the certificate again before filing it away. Odd that I should have overlooked her occupation. Somehow, I hadn't imagined her having one. She had been an artist.

THE SUN

'Well, this is a bit more cheerful, isn't it, Dorothy – an artist, eh. Good for you. This definitely merits a celebration. I've brought you some bleach. It's about time your headstone stood out from the crowd.'

Turning to Eleanor, I handed her a pair of Marigolds. 'Off you go.'

'You're mad,' she said. 'Oh, what did I do to deserve such a mad mother? Do I have to wear them?'

'Yes,' I replied emphatically. 'I don't want you catching anything unpleasant. Now, just see if you can get rid of that horrible green slime. You scrub away and I'll chuck the water on. I'm sorry, Eleanor, I'd do it myself -'

'Yes, yes, I know, your hands. So, after I've finished, can I go over to Milly's?'

'I should think so, yes, as long as her mother brings you home by nine. Now, as your reward, I thought I'd treat you to a trip to London at the weekend. You could invite Milly, if you like. We could go to the Imperial War Museum.'

'Oh, Mum, do we have to? We've been there loads of times. I really don't think Dorothy did any artwork for the War Effort.'

'No, I think there's a very good chance she did. People with skills were expected to use them during the War; and I'm sure Dorothy wasn't the type to sit at home doing nothing. She'll have wanted to do her bit.'

'Yes, I'm sure somebody gave her plenty of work to do. All right then, so what am I supposed to do with this wire wool?'

'Just see if you can get inside the letters. It doesn't have to be perfect. Just spruce it up a bit. Yes, that's the idea. Your Nana would be proud of you.'

'No she wouldn't; she'd call Social Services.'

'Oh, I don't know about that, Eleanor. You know how she feels about Dorothy's inscription. Yes, wouldn't it be nice if we could get hold of one of Dorothy's paintings, or a print or something, to show Nana. She'd love that, wouldn't she?'

'She might. But then she's never been very keen on your paintings, so I don't see why you think she'd be that fussed about Dorothy's. She's not an Art lover.'

'She liked that portrait I did of you.'

'Yes, but that's the only one. I wonder if Dorothy painted portraits. I expect you're hoping she did.'

'Oh, I'm not sure about that!'

'Why don't you ask her while we're here, see if she can arrange for you to see a self-portrait?'

I laughed, 'Come on, speed it up a bit. Less chat, more elbow grease.'

And off she went. She did a grand job, I must say, and by the time she'd finished, Dorothy was gleaming in the afternoon sun. Pronouncing myself highly-satisfied, I drove Eleanor to her friend's house, then sped off to the library, intent on tracking down some evidence of Dorothy's artistic career.

With any luck, the archives would yield - if not a portrait - a nicely-composed still life executed in a figurative style. Somehow, I couldn't imagine Dorothy as an Abstract Expressionist or Conceptualist; dismembering pregnant cows, urinating into a bottle, or even winning a glittering prize for her astonishingly luminous and thought-provoking collage: 'Yesterday's Knickers with Ten French Letters and a Twisted Bra Strap.' It was always possible, of course, that Dorothy had been ahead of her time. She certainly seemed to have a peculiar relationship with time; but I had no reason to suppose that she had been a Futurist *before* she died. True, I did not yet have her Horoscope; but I would have been very surprised had it yielded the signature of, say, a Jackson Pollock or a Damien Hurst. Had it done so, of course, it would have made life a lot easier because then she would have been famous, and I could have downloaded her from the Internet instead of bothering poor old Martin, the Friendly Librarian, yet again. Not that the badge he wore pinned to his chest said, 'Martin, the Friendly Librarian.' It just said, 'Martin.'

'It's a management initiative,' he said giving me a wry smile.

'Really?'

'We're supposed to be dispelling the public image of librarians as dysfunctional introverts.'

'Oh, is that the public image of librarians? Oh, well, Martin; my name's Gwendolen, I'm a dysfunctional introvert and I'm very pleased to meet you.'

Smiling, I held out my be-gloved hand. I liked Martin. He had a gentle familiarity which wasn't intrusive. He had a calm and sympathetic outer manner. He probably had Libra Rising and was either happily married or gay.

'I remember you,' he said. 'You're the woman with the mysterious grave, although I must say, you don't strike me as particularly introverted - especially not in that hat.'

'I made it,' I said proudly, 'If you like, I'll knit you one as well. That should give the public a different image of librarians.'

'Yes, I'm sure it would. So, how can I help you today? Did you have any joy with the parish register? You certainly seem in a very good mood.'

'I am,' I chirped happily. 'I'm in a very good mood. I haven't felt this cheerful for quite a while. Now, you're going to love this. I've got excellent news with regard to Dorothy. Oh, yes, I'm hot on the trail now. She's come out of the closet. My daughter found her in the parish register.'

'Oh, good for her. So it wasn't the wrong surname then?'

'No. They put the wrong date on the inscription, not the wrong name. She was who I thought she was and nobody else.'

'That must have come as a relief.'

'Oh, it did. I can assure you. It came as a great relief. Yes, it was the wrong year. Dorothy died in 1946.'

'Ah,' he nodded, 'I should have thought of that. It's not unusual for stonemasons to make a mistake with the date.'

'Oh, it wasn't the stonemason,' I replied. 'It was Peter.'

'Peter?'

'Yes, you know: "to you the stars, narcissi fields and music." Him. Now, I think the headstone went up some time after she died, possibly several years, and, in the interval, he'd forgotten the date. Well, that wouldn't be unusual, would it? People do get very mixed up about dates. And when you consider, there were a lot of displaced persons around at the time.'

'Displaced persons?'

'Yes, just after the War. He could have been taken prisoner and only found out that Dorothy had died when he came home. I imagine that kind of thing happened quite often. My mother was a nurse in the War and she says it did. You'd think they'd gone, and they would suddenly turn up. But not always, of course.'

'Ah, yes, I see what you mean now. But you'd have thought her husband would have got the correct date, wouldn't you? Or that a relative would have informed him.'

'Oh, Peter wasn't her husband,' I said. 'Not unless it was her nickname for him, which I don't think it was. No, her husband was called Wilfrid.' Reaching into my pocket, I brought out her Death Certificate and placed it on his desk. 'There you are, that's him. He registered her death.'

'Well, well, your mystery deepens.'

'Doesn't it. Of course, I shan't rest until I've found out who Peter was. But, for the time being, it's Dorothy I'm after. I want to find something she painted and this is where I was hoping you could help because it turns out she was an artist. And that's another coincidence – although I wouldn't call myself an artist as such - my house is full of paintings, most of them mine.'

'Really?' he appeared puzzled and began scratching his beard. This was not a good sign. Perhaps I had overwhelmed him? I decided to tone it down.

'Of course, unlike Dorothy,' I quickly added, 'I'm not an artist by profession. I'm an astrologer and I teach History in my spare time.'

This seemed to surprise him – or was there something else wrong? For he was now sucking in his cheeks as if digesting something difficult. I hoped I hadn't erred in mentioning Astrology, which can often elicit strange reactions from people who are otherwise friendly and polite.

'Is anything the matter?' I asked.

He hesitated. 'Well – it's just that you said she was an artist.'

'That's right. She was. Look, there it is: under Occupation, it says, 'Artist.'

'Um.' This time he scratched the tip of his nose. 'Yes, I can see how you might have missed this.'

'Sorry?'

'I'm surprised they did that as late as forty-six. Oh, well, they obviously did.'

'Did what?'

'Cited the husband's occupation on the wife's death certificate – not very P.C. is it.'

'What? Oh, no. She was an artist. Look, it says, 'Occupation,' then it says, 'Wife of Wilfrid Browning,' yes, but then there's a gap, and then it says, 'Artist.'

'Yes,' he said patiently. 'He was an artist. Her occupation, I'm afraid, was, 'Wife of Wilfrid.'

'Oh, no!'

'I'm afraid so.'

'But that's not an occupation.'

'It was in those days,' he replied. 'Still is, I should think, for a lot of women.'

I groaned, 'Oh, God, you're right, aren't you, and I've got it wrong again! I don't think, that's my trouble, I just leap straight in. Oh, what an idiot. How stupid can you get? Of course, you're right. It's obvious now you've pointed it out. My mother will have a field day with this.'

'Well, I wouldn't be too hard on yourself,' he said kindly. 'It's an easy enough mistake to make. But, listen, Dorothy could well have been an artist in her own right too. Shall we have a try?'

But I knew before we set off that we weren't going to find Dorothy in the Catalogue of Artists. We did, however, find Wilfrid Browning without any difficulty. He had exhibited twice in Oxford before the First World War: at Exeter College in 1911, and again in 1913: 'the College Chapel,' and the 'Rector's Hall.'

'Perhaps he was religious,' I said.

'I wonder?' said Martin. 'It's rather odd there's no record of him painting after that. When was the last one, 1913? He could well have been wounded in action.'

'He could have been,' I said. 'But maybe he exhibited somewhere else? They were living in London when she died.'

'Ah, he may have joined up there.'

'Or he may not have joined up at all.'

'I'd have thought that unlikely, wouldn't you? But while we're here, shall we have a look? We can certainly try the local regimental records, though if he joined up in London, it'll be harder. A lot of their records are incomplete.'

'Why not,' I said; although since I wasn't especially interested in Wilfrid's career, I wasn't disappointed when we couldn't find it. Martin, however, had now become quite enthusiastic; and began putting forward various theories to explain why Wilfrid may have stopped painting after World War One, which ranged from losing his sight to losing his spirit.

'If he was religious,' he said, 'as these entries suggest, he may have lost his Faith during the War. Didn't they say God died on the first day of the Somme?'

'They did,' I replied. 'But Wilfrid was still an artist on Dorothy's Death Certificate and that was after the Second World War.'

'Ah, yes, of course. But it would still be interesting, wouldn't it, to see whether his paintings changed after the First World War. It must have had an impact. You could try some of the London libraries.'

'I could,' I agreed. 'Maybe I'll do that. It would make a change from burial records.'

As he closed the catalogue, he gave me a sympathetic look. 'You're really disappointed by this, aren't you?'

'Am I? I don't know. I suppose I am. She didn't have a very good death, you see, so I was hoping she'd have had a wonderful life; painting and doing what she loved, because I have this feeling she didn't have any children.'

He nodded thoughtfully. 'She may still have had a wonderful life.'

'Well, I hope so.'

'Tell you what,' he said, 'we're not busy at the moment; I'll give you a hand. There should be a record of their marriage.'

I didn't reply at once. I wasn't interested in their marriage - although I was becoming mildly interested in my lack of interest in their marriage.

'It's very kind of you,' I said.

'It'll give you her maiden name,' he added.

At this, I perked up, 'Oh, of course. But won't it be difficult? I don't want to waste any more of your time.'

'No, no. It's no trouble and I know a short cut.'

Happily, this meant I didn't have to spend hours ploughing through the Index. Martin found the announcement of their marriage in the Newspaper Archive within the space of ten minutes.

On August 14th 1926, at St. Giles Church: Wilfrid George; only son of Mr and Mrs C. Browning married Dorothy Margaret, only daughter of Mrs Carter and Mr G. Baker deceased.

'Well, that's interesting,' I said, 'That's not the church where's she's buried. She must have moved at some point. Well, thank you very much, Martin, you've been a great help.'

Informed, now, of her maiden name, it didn't take me long to locate the record of her birth. It didn't surprise me – and this was the highlight of my afternoon – to discover that Dorothy's had been a summer birth. Although I did not yet have the exact date (her birth had been registered in the September Quarter) I felt sure that she had been a Leo: proud, noble, steadfast and warm. A little managerial, perhaps, with a slight tendency to interfere in the lives of others; but, overall, well-meaning.

On my way home from the library, I called in at my allotment, picked the last of the season's sunflowers, and took them down to Dorothy's grave.

'You were a Leo, weren't you, Dorothy. A sunny, creative Leo, born to shine. You were a Leo yet you married an artist. Now, I find that very interesting. Did you shine for yourself, or for someone else?'.

When I was a child, I shone for my father. I shone because my father was blinded in the War and it was my job to cheer him up. After all, as my grandmother told me, I was, his 'Little Eyes.'

And I loved this name. I loved my job. I felt proud. It was an honour. How I loved to walk out with my father, leading him by the hand. More than anything in the world, I wanted to bring my father out of the darkness; and so I carefully concealed from him anything I knew would disturb him. He had suffered enough. He must never suffer again, and especially not through me. So I went round him as a small child shining: always cheerful, always sunny.

I would give him the pictures I painted.. And he would run his hands across the surface. 'Ah, yes,' he would say, 'You have really captured the sunrise.. You have really captured the light.'

Oh, yes, I loved my job. And I loved my father. He was a generous man. 'I have every confidence in you,' he always said.

But when he died, I knew that I had failed. I was his 'Little Eyes' but I didn't see it coming.. He died alone and afraid.

Oh, but we are in this chapter under the benevolent and warming rays of the Sun: we really ought to close on a cheerful note. But it wasn't a cheerful summer. Bill was marrying his twin. My mother suffered a further stroke.

Try. Try harder.

Well, we did have a week with my cousin in the Pyrenees. Trouble was, my skin got worse. The heat didn't help.

Keep at it. We are going to end this chapter on a cheerful note. It doesn't have to be brilliant. What about Dorothy? You said you thought she was a Leo, so was she?

Well, yes, but I didn't find that out until later.

Never mind. Include it now.

All right then. Yes, she was. I was right. And her Leo Sun conjoined my Ascendant. She had seen me that day in the churchyard, recognised something in me. I didn't know what, but I did know: it was meant to be.

THE MOON

The Sun was in Libra, the Moon in Virgo, and Uranus in Aquarius ascended on Thursday, the 7th of October, when Eleanor, on her thirteenth birthday, opened what she took to be another greetings card only to pull out Dorothy's Birth Certificate instead. 'That's a bit much,' she said. 'I was hoping for some vouchers from Uncle Dan. Oh.'

Alerted by her sudden change of tone, I paused en route to the kitchen with my shopping and gave her a quizzical look.

'You're not going to like this, Mum. Maybe you should sit down.'

'Sit down – whatever for?'

'It's Dorothy – she was born in Bill's road.'

'Oh, I don't believe it, let me see.'

She was right, of course. 'Oh, my God.' I fell back into the armchair, dropping my shopping and dislodging a sleeping cat.

Rising from the floor, she gathered up her cards and rescued the cat. 'Oh, come on Mum,' she said. 'Look on the bright side. She could have been born in Bill's house and then she would have had to spend the Afterlife cleaning.' And with that pithy remark, she retired to her bedroom, leaving me to recover my equilibrium alone - and prepare the Birthday Tea.

Just as I was putting the finishing touches to the trifle, the doorbell rang, heralding the arrival of her friends; shortly followed by my oldest friend, Joanna, who'd driven up from London bearing gifts. 'Where is she? Where's the Birthday Girl?' She called out whereupon Eleanor and her little troop of girlfriends tumbled downstairs to receive their treats then ran back up again.

'We've got another Birthday Girl in here, Jo,' I said, beckoning her into the kitchen where I brought her up to date with my news as we laid out the spread and drank tea.

'Well, I don't know what to make of it, Gwen,' she said, covering the sandwiches with cling film. 'The whole thing's extremely strange.'

'You can say that again,' I replied, popping another pizza into the oven.

'Could there be another road in Oxford with the same name?'

'Unfortunately, no. Dorothy's got Bill for a neighbour whether she likes it or not. Yes, of all the yellow-bricked, Victorian villas she could have chosen, why did she have to choose the one opposite his? Well, of course, this means I can't go and make my pilgrimage now to her Birthplace in case I bump into Them.'

Wiping out the fruit bowl, she began filling it with crisps. 'I suppose you could always go during the night – or in disguise. You could wear a false moustache and the opera cloak you got from the Oxfam shop.'

'I could,' I laughed. 'Yes, that would give the neighbours something to worry about. But no. I don't want to risk seeing them again, Jo. It's too much. Dorothy's Birthplace will have to wait.'

'So, how long for do you think?'

'Oh, I don't know. I imagine I'll feel better after they're married. That'll put the seal on things - make it more real.'

'You still think that's going to happen?'

'I should think so. I know you don't.'

'No, it never works between twins, I don't think. They fall in love with themselves in a kind of sleep; and when they wake up, they start finding fault with one another. And when that happens – with Bill and his twin – that's when you'll need to be ready, stronger in yourself and clearer about what you want.'

Opening the fridge, I brought out the cheesecake and gave it a tap with the back of a spoon.

'Well, it wouldn't do you any harm now, would it,' she continued, 'to think about what you need. Would you want him back after this?'

'I haven't been thinking along those lines because I don't think it's going to happen.'

'Ah, so you do want him back.'

At times like this, I wondered whether Joanna might have Scorpio Ascendant. Her appearance suggested the Moon rising with Venus in Virgo: she had warm brown eyes, a heart-shaped face and olive skin; yet she could be very penetrating – and persistent.

'You really have got to think about what you want, you know, Gwen, because it's not going to work out between Bill and his missing twin. Oh, it was all very well in the summer, while he was out there having fun, but he won't want a free spirit when the nights draw further in, he'll want apple crumble and his washing done. Can't see a free spirit doing that can you? He doesn't need a twin, Bill, actually, he needs a wealthy patron. Yes, maybe we can find him one before he turns up on your doorstep with his laundry. Unless you want him back, of course.'

I looked up at the calendar on my kitchen wall; the image, a forest of maple trees shedding their leaves. 'Oh, I don't know what I want, Jo, to be honest. I do miss him, but I really don't think he'll be back, even if it doesn't work out with his twin. He wasn't happy with me, remember. I pushed him away, he said; and I didn't see him. Well, maybe I didn't.'

'You foresaw him,' she said after a while. 'Saw what he might be. We all do it.'

After she had gone - and the girls, tucked up in sleeping bags, watched a video in the front room - I went into my cupboard under the stairs and brought out his photograph.

'Oh, I don't know, Bill,' I said, 'I'm not sure that I didn't see you, really. There were lots of things I saw in you and loved. Your sense of humour, of course, which is second to none; your intelligence, and interest in things being fair. So, oh, I don't know.'

Yet, I knew there had been some truth in what he'd said, for if I had seen him clearly, I wouldn't have spent so much time trying to fathom him out. Returning his photograph, I next brought out his Speculative Horoscope, recalling the investigation I had mounted in my attempt to find his correct time of birth, even suggesting that his younger sister might try hypnosis.

Much as I liked her, I'd felt especially frustrated with Lynne, because she had taken up Astrology in her youth and had actually drawn up his chart, but couldn't remember the first thing about it, apart from: it 'described him rather well.' She had then said she had come to doubt it because their mother had been somewhat absent-minded, and couldn't remember whether the original time she had given had been the correct one after all. Could it have been lunchtime, or teatime? She had the feeling there was a meal involved. But then again, it could have been breakfast or supper or a late evening snack. At one point, she had a feeling for Gemini. Aha, I thought, the twins. But shortly afterwards, she'd changed her mind. In the end, I had decided I would have to rectify the chart.

Now, this is a long and complicated procedure, which involves matching planetary alignments to the key events in a person's life. It also involves some difficult Maths which, at the best of times, I do not enjoy. The hardest part, of course, is getting people to tell you the truth about their key events; and given Bill's scepticism of Astrology, not to mention his somewhat secretive nature, I hadn't expected too much success on this front. Nevertheless, I'd employed all my powers of persuasion.

'Go on, indulge me,' I'd said, 'just this once.'

I was wearing my black velvet dress. I had cooked a wonderful meal. The evening was young. And by the end of it, the Key Events of Bill's Life ran to thirteen sides of A4.

And here they were still, neatly tucked inside a padded envelope. Smiling, I pulled them out, thoroughly enjoying this trip down Memory Lane, and laughing at the comments he had written in the margins.

First Love? Aged sixteen. (Peaked early)

Childhood Illnesses? (Too many to mention)

Operations? (Did an in-growing toe nail count?)

Various academic qualifications were followed by a long list of women's names:

Lorna, Jennifer, Kathleen, Sally (Same generation)

Melanie, Hannah, Rebecca (Getting younger by the minute)

Ali, Toni, Vic and Trish (Shorter too).

So, I had asked him, could he remember when we first met?

'No,' he'd replied. 'Can you?'

Sadly, I could not.

But he had remembered the exact time and place when he had met Naomi, the brilliant and beautiful mathematician, who had left him for the City of London before we met up again. And not only the details but how he had felt. And there it was, in my own handwriting: at ten minutes past two in the afternoon of July 11th 1994, in the King's Arms. Instant Recognition.

July 11th?

I felt the temperature in the room drop. I looked up at the door and glanced around the room. No, no one there, I was imagining things. Lifting my cardigan from the back of my chair, I wrapped it around my shoulders and returned to the list. How on earth could I have overlooked this at the time? I knew very well that I had discovered Dorothy's grave before I became an astrologer, yet there was nothing to suggest I had made the connection. Could I have made a mistake and written July instead of June? That didn't seem unlikely. After all, I still had a long way to go before meeting my mother's standards – a hell of a long way, I realised, as I opened my diary. Yes, I had forgotten to record the date Bill met Madeleine. So, what was it he'd said now, the night I met up with him, the night of my dream? 'A fortnight ago, give or take a day or two on either side.' And I had met him on July 24th. Close. Close enough. So, what had I been doing on the 11th? 'Eczema flared up,' was all it said. Oh, right. Bill, had been out and about in broad daylight falling in love with his twin, and what was I doing on Dorothy's anniversary? Rotting.

Closing my diary, I rubbed my eyes then gazed at my reflection in the window pane. 'You can read too much into these things,' I told myself. 'It doesn't mean anything.' So, why did I feel like crying? Who was this pathetic creature gazing blankly into a pane of glass feeling sorry for herself? Surely not me. And, really, there was no need. Bill would not have chosen that particular day on purpose. He didn't believe in Fate; he didn't believe in

Coincidence. There were three hundred and sixty five days in the year, and they were all the same to him. So, I pushed it away, the sad and lonely thought: they were all the same to him, but not to me.

After this discovery I experienced a marked loss of interest in Dorothy's story. A couple of days later, her Marriage Certificate arrived in the post. I did not go charging off to St Giles Church with a bunch of red roses. Nor did I erect a chart for this event. It could have been the Gas Bill landing on the doormat for all I cared. I opened the envelope, noted its contents then filed it away. In the same period, Wilfrid's Birth Certificate arrived. So, he had been a Capricorn - so what? Again, I noted the contents and filed it away. October drew to its close, without my opening my Ephemeris, visiting Dorothy's grave or entering a single event in my diary until one day towards the end of the month, I drove down to Wales to visit my mother - who reminded me before I could even sit down.

'Have you brought me your next chapter?' she demanded.

'No. I've brought you some coconut creams. You like those. And I baked you a cake.'

'A cake? What's got into you? I don't want a cake. I want another chapter. I want to see you finish something.

I can still read you know. Well, you can put it in the post when you get back. Now, have you got a pen and paper? I want you to make an inventory.'

'But, Mum, why?'

'In case I move, of course. I don't want them thinking I've taken anything that doesn't belong to me.'

'Oh, Mum, do we have to? I've just driven for hours and I'm feeling a bit shaky.'

'All the more reason to do something useful then so you can get your bearings.'

'All right. All right.'

Fortunately, Eleanor had already produced an exercise book and was carefully logging every movable item in the room. This felt completely insane. It also felt reassuringly normal. At last, my mother declared herself satisfied and ready for her trip to the sea front where she had great fun hurtling along the promenade in her wheelchair with Eleanor at the helm.

'Oh, you're no fun,' she said when I suggested we head back; and turned to give Eleanor a conspiratorial smile: 'She's no fun, is she, your mother. Come on, Nell, let's have one more go. Just you and me. One more for the road.'

But I could see she was getting tired and feeling the cold; shivering under her tartan blanket and clutching her handbag full of sweets.

'We should go back now,' I repeated.

But she shook her head anxiously, 'No, not yet. Oh why are you always in such a hurry? You must allow me to collect my thoughts.'

This was no longer easy for her to do; and it was the hardest thing for me to watch, the struggle she had with her memory. Where had it gone? She hadn't lost it completely. I imagined it had just moved house. For her eyes were wet with memory; they were drenched with memory therefore it could not have gone for good.

'Just give me another minute, Gwendolen, please.'

So, we waited: watching the clouds, watching the swell of the sea and the swooping gulls while she plucked at the sleeve of her cardigan. This would take quite some time.

At last she brightened, 'I knew it. I knew there was something.'

And slipping her good hand into her pocket, she brought out a small calling card: Dorothy's inscription.

'Now, this is important. Don't think me critical but you made a mistake. It's <u>for</u> you the stars, narcissi fields and music; not <u>to</u> you, which is what you wrote in your Neptune chapter. Promise me you'll change it.'

'Yes, yes, don't worry.'

'You won't forget?'

'No, I'll do it as soon as I get back.'

'Because it's very important, Gwendolen. It's essential to get the details right.'

'Yes, Mum. Don't worry. I won't forget.'

I didn't have the heart to tell her that, on this occasion, she had got the details wrong. Nor did I have the heart to tell her that Dorothy wasn't Welsh. It didn't seem to matter now that she'd come home.

'All right then.' I nodded for Eleanor to release the brakes. But as she did so, my mother lurched forward and grabbed my wrist.

'I wanted to write,' she said, pressing it into me. 'I wanted to write.'

'You did, Mum,' I said, remembering her diaries. 'You always did.'

'She'll be all right,' said Eleanor as we began the journey home. 'She's got Uncle Dan, and Auntie Alison, and the Girls. She'll be fine once she's settled in.'

I nodded and swallowed the urge to cry. She wasn't coming back: I knew that now, and life was going to be very different without my mother around the corner, recording my every deed and going through my bank statements with a red pen. For her too. What would she do with her time now that she could no longer wield a pen? All her papers, notebooks, diaries, I now kept. And I had left her with a handbag full of sweets.

Having spent the best part of four hours at the wheel returning from Wales (thanks to road-works on the M4 and high winds on the Severn Bridge) I was really hoping for a lazy Sunday afternoon at home the next day, but no such luck. Just as I was settling down with a milky coffee and a good read, my mother rang on her new telephone demanding that I go down to Dorothy's grave and tidy it up.

'It's Halloween,' she announced (as if she had been a lifelong pagan).

'Yes, I know.'

'Well, according to your beliefs, it's the Festival of the Dead. So I thought you could kill two birds with one stone: go and pay your respects and do what needs to be done before the winter. I know you've been neglecting it, Gwendolen. You can't pull the wool over my eyes. You haven't been down there for ages, I know.'

'Mum, you don't believe in Life after Death.'

'No, but you do. Now, I've said my piece, I shall leave you get on with it.'

'Better do as you're told, Mum,' said Eleanor, peering over her magazine.

So, gathering up my tools, I went. And not in a very good mood, I should add: at the tender age of forty-two, I was still taking orders from my mother; my wheelbarrow had a dodgy tyre; and my garden shears (which I'd left out in the rain) were covered in rust. But as luck would have it, it turned out I wouldn't need them.

When I got to the churchyard, I found that someone had beaten me to it. Someone had beaten a path through the nettles; laying - by way of stepping stones - a trail of broken up cardboard boxes which stopped about a foot short of grave. Meanwhile, the earth had been freshly dug; and a jam jar containing a single rose sat propped against the headstone, wedged between two stones.

'Well. Who's been visiting my grave?' I said. 'Come on, Dorothy, what's going on here? Have you got a secret admirer, or what? Because if you have, I think I should be told.'

No response.

'Oh, come on Dorothy,' I repeated, tapping my forehead, 'Who is it? Who, apart from me, would visit your grave? It's not as though you've got any relatives, is it? Well, not that I know of. And you are a bit off the beaten track down here. So, what's going on, I wonder? Come on, Dorothy. Who is it? Who's the interloper? Who, apart from me, has been visiting your grave?'

As far as I could remember, I hadn't told too many people about Dorothy's grave. Excluding family members (as suspects) my list comprised: Bill, Joanna, two vicars and an archivist; Martin, the Friendly Librarian, and Lily who fed the churchyard cats. I may have mentioned it - in passing - to a handful of teaching colleagues; and I had certainly mentioned it to my astrological pen friend, Richard, many times. However, he lived north of Birmingham; and I could hardly see Richard, keen gardener though he was, nipping down to Oxford for an afternoon of churchyard clearance. Neither could I quite imagine Bill, who had enough trouble managing his own unwieldy garden, in that role. No, much as I enjoyed the image of Bill thrashing his way through the nettles with his grandfather's rusty old scythe, I didn't think it very likely. On the other hand, in a certain mood, he might consider it rather a good joke - and he did live very close by. I looked again at the single rose. Could this be a sign that all was no longer blissful in the twin bed, and could this be his way of letting me know? Not that he had ever given me a red rose, but he had once given me a bag of seed potatoes and a bunch of daffs.

Oh, what the hell, why not, I thought, as I left the churchyard to cross the road; it was worth a try. She might be in, she might not be; but surely after all this time, I ought to be able to face them at home. Even so, my pulse was racing as I knocked on the front door.

I needn't have worried. She wasn't in. Nor did I detect the slightest hint of a female presence as I followed him down the dark and narrow hallway into the kitchen. His grandfather's chair was piled high, as always, with student essays, journals and newspapers. Several black bags containing washing sat stubbornly on the quarry-tiled floor like guests who refused to go home; and the sink was brimming over with crockery.

'I don't suppose you've been visiting my grave, have you?' I said, shifting some papers to make myself comfortable.

'Not yet, no. Cup of tea?'

'Yes, please. Only someone has, and it isn't me.'

'How very strange, and you suspect me?'

'Well, I did think it was the sort of thing you might do on a whim.'

'No, if it were up to me, I'd have you cremated. Sugar?'

'No, thanks. Well, if it wasn't you, I wonder who it was. It's very odd.'

'Yes,' he said, giving me a cryptic look. 'Isn't it.'

'I suppose it could have been Martin,' I said vaguely.

'Martin?'

'Martin, the Friendly Librarian. He's been helping me out with my research.'

'Has he indeed?'

'Yes, but I doubt it was him, actually. He looks pretty normal to me.'

'Not the man for you then.'

'Oh, no, Bill, I'm not interested in him in that way. I just like him, that's all. I told him about my mystical experience and he's become quite interested. It was thanks to him I found Wilfrid.'

'Wilfrid? Martin? Could this be the same One Man Woman? Really, Gwendolen, you have been busy. I should leave you more often.'

At this, his face clouded over. I could see him almost bite his lip. According to his version of events, I had left him whereas from my point of view, it was the other way around. I didn't challenge this, however, because I didn't want an argument; and, besides, he quickly moved the conversation on. Soon we were chatting, just like old times, about College, the allotment and my research. Familiar stuff, really. But it was nice. I felt we could still be friends. Before I left, I asked if he could call in at Exeter on my behalf and enquire about Wilfrid's paintings since he knew someone who worked there.

'Mind you, it'll probably turn out to be another red herring,' I said, waving him goodbye.

By now, there had been so many peculiar twists in the tale of Dorothy Browning, it wouldn't have surprised me if her husband's long-lost masterpieces had been destroyed by an art-hating militant atheist: after all, he had painted, 'the Rector's Hall' and 'the College Chapel.' What did surprise me was that Bill got in touch again so soon: the same evening in fact.

The Sun was in Scorpio, the Moon in Leo and Cancer ascended, placing a powerful Mars in Capricorn on the opposite cusp when Bill telephoned to advise me that I had probably got a stalker. He had been thinking, he said, about the strange business of the unknown visitor to Dorothy's grave, and had reached the conclusion that I could be in danger, especially since a woman had recently been attacked in the churchyard.

'Really?' I said. 'I haven't heard about that.'

'I believe it was in the papers,' he replied. 'But then you don't read the papers, or watch the local news. Then again, it may have been hearsay. Either way, my point is that a woman was attacked in the churchyard and the assailant hasn't been caught, so I'm suggesting you be more careful. I wouldn't go down there alone if I were you, at least for the time being. I don't want to bury you yet.'

'You don't want to bury me at all,' I retorted, 'You'd have me cremated.'

'Will you listen, I'm being serious. You know, for someone so neurotic you can be remarkably reckless at times – which is par for the course, I suppose.'

'I know I can be reckless, Bill,' I replied, 'but I promise you nothing bad is going to happen to me while I'm visiting Dorothy's grave. I feel perfectly safe there. For me, it's sacred ground.'

'Yes, yes. But let's assume this stalker doesn't know that, shall we? Let's assume he doesn't know about the mystic emanations that unaccountably arise from Dorothy's grave. For him you are just an ordinary woman - albeit possessed of certain Venusian charms - he doesn't know you, remember. No, for him, you're an easy target; and he remains blissfully unaware - as he lunges from his stake-out in the bushes - that's he's about to incur the wrath of God. Or, he may not care. Damned for all eternity, he thinks, but worth it.'

'Oh, stop it,' I laughed. 'Of course I haven't got a stalker. You're winding me up.'

'No, I'm not. It is possible that you've been watched.'

'All right then, Bill, if I've got a stalker - which I don't believe I have - why would he leave a neat little trail of cardboard for me to walk on – unless he's Walter Raleigh and he thinks I'm Good Queen Bess. Well, it's hardly the action of a maniac, is it? In fact, it's rather a thoughtful thing to do.'

'Oh, no doubt he has his tender loving side. Or he could be trying to win your confidence, to soften you up before he moves in for the kill. We don't know his motives. What we do know is that the churchyard isn't a safe place for a woman at the moment. We know this for a fact.'

'All right,' I softened. 'I'll take more care.' Although I had no intention of changing my habits, I appreciated his concern. 'Thank you,' I added.

'You're very welcome.'

But he didn't sound too anxious to sign off. 'So, what are you up to at the moment? Writing your memoirs, I suppose.'

'No; it's Halloween.'

'Ah, so you'll be out there communing with your ancestors.'

'I will be, at some point. Then again, I might have visitors.'

'Women only?'

'If you haven't got anything better to do, Bill, by all means come round.'

I always celebrate Halloween. It's the only Festival I observe apart from Christmas. On Christmas Eve, I go to Midnight Mass. On Halloween, I bring out the family photographs, and recite all their names - as my grandmother taught me – which was what I was doing when Bill arrived.

'Well now,' he said, sniffing the air in my kitchen. 'What have you got brewing in this pot: eye of newt, toe of Philosopher?'

'It's punch,' I replied. 'Help yourself.'

'Thank you, I will. Well, I must say, this isn't like you, Gwendolen, drinking alone. Come to think of it, you don't drink. Are you expecting someone else?'

'It's Halloween. You never know who's going to call round.'

'Hmm. Where's Eleanor?'

'Over at Milly's. But what is this, Bill, the Spanish Inquisition?'

'No, I just have this feeling you were expecting me. You see, I can't help thinking you saw this coming.'

'Oh, but you don't believe it,' I said. 'You don't believe in Astrology and you don't believe in the Supernatural.'

'I don't have to <u>believe</u> in Astrology to find it interesting. It isn't a matter of belief.'

I was about to reply but he suddenly looked so miserable, I decided it probably wasn't a good time to launch an argument about the Meaning of Life.

'You'll tell me, I suppose,' he said, sinking back down into the old armchair, 'You'll tell me, I'm sure, it's Neptune.' Then he told me the sad story of how his dream dissolved. It had all begun to unravel when they returned from their holiday in the Sun: when the time had come to make it real, she had cut and run. For this was her pattern: when people got too close, she ran away. She felt safer that way. She had returned to her previous lover who would never really be there for her; she had chosen the past.

I nodded then reached for my cigarettes. 'That does sound like Neptune.'

'Absent Father Syndrome,' he said. 'Another one.'

'I haven't got an absent father.'

'Yes, you have.'

'No, I haven't. He's dead, it's true. But he isn't absent.'

'He must be, or he wouldn't haunt you.'

'He doesn't haunt me. He's safely tucked away in a far and distant land.'

'A Land Fit for Heroes?'

'Well, who knows? Who knows about that?'

'I know,' he replied. 'There is no Land Fit for Heroes in this world – which is why you must carve one out for him in the stars.'

I reached for my glass of punch, 'Is that right?'

'I think so. It's why you became an astrologer. Oh, you tried History at first, looking for answers: Why him? Why did he have to suffer? But History proved a disappointment. No consolation there. So, next you turned to the Imaginal Realms. I can create, you thought; I can re-create the Land Fit for Heroes he deserved but never got. And where better to look than to the stars - where no one can prove you wrong, and where you can remain forever his golden child, ever on the look-out. It's why you never finish anything that matters to you. And why you always feel alone.'

I took another sip of punch. 'Well, that's an interesting perspective, but you know I've never been very keen on psychological explanations. They reduce people, I think.'

'On the contrary.' He lit another cigarette. 'Yes, I haven't forgotten the painting you showed me when we first met; the one you made the night your father died, a small child looking out to sea in the dead of night. No stars in that sky.'

'Oh, I haven't got that one anymore,' I said. 'I painted over it. But never mind my father, Bill. Shouldn't you be asking yourself why you're always attracted to women with absent fathers?'

'That's easy,' he replied, 'I'm a mirror.'

'You're always saying that.'

'Yes, because I am.'

'Hmm, well, I don't know about mirrors.'

'No, because you're not one.'

'I really don't understand what you mean.'

He shrugged. 'When you're a mirror, people look at you and they see themselves.'

I remembered my dream: a mirror in the hallway, the crystal chandelier and how quickly I had taken myself out of that scenario; wanting to make good my escape. Maybe I didn't want to be seen? On the other hand, it did make very good sense to steer well clear of breaking glass, to keep well out of it.

'Well, I'm sorry it hasn't worked out as you hoped, Bill,' I said, preparing to clear up. But he followed me out to the kitchen and buttered a slice of bread.

'Now, you're not going to tell me you didn't see this coming. I won't allow you that.'

'I didn't as a matter of fact.'

'You must have looked at your charts.'

'I didn't look for an outcome. No point.'

'But you knew there was this Neptune going on.'

'Yes, but it doesn't cause anything. The planets are signs not causes. For some people the dream comes true. You can't tell from a Birth Chart what people are going to do with it. You can only speculate, you can't predict.'

'But you ought to be able to predict - if there's anything in it.'

'I don't think so. Astrology doesn't work like that. If it did, astrologers would be extremely rich. It's not mechanical thing, it's an Art. There's something else going on.'

'Oh, yes.' He gave a wry smile. 'With you, there always is.'

'You get to see what's permitted,' I replied. 'What you need to know.'

'Is that so?'

'I'm not a hundred per cent sure, but that's my feeling.'

'But you will be able to predict, I'm sure, where the Sun will be in about six months from now.'

I hesitated, not quite following his drift.

'You've got your Ephemeris. You can predict exactly where the Sun will be - and all the other planets. So, where will it be, the Sun, in early May or thereabouts?'

'The Sun, in May? Well, Taurus -

'She's pregnant,' he said.

And, no, I didn't cast the chart for this announcement. I was too busy throwing-up in the kitchen sink to look at the clock.

'I'm sorry about all this,' said Bill as he helped me clean up: 'It's a terrible mess, I know.'

'It's the alcohol,' I replied, 'I'm not used to it.'

My next few diary entries flatly state: ill. Throat. Stomach. By the 6th of November, however, I must have recovered, for I now enjoyed a, 'lovely meal with Bill and Eleanor,' at the White Hart in Wytham. On the 16th, Bill mended the downstairs loo and replaced light fittings; on the 24th, he cleaned out the guttering and repaired a broken chair. We spent Christmas with his sisters in Yorkshire. I spent the New Year with my mother. There are no further entries during this period, apart from the usual: 'Skin bad again. Feet.' Then, on the 6th of January 2000, I telephoned an astrologer in London with a question that had been on my mind for some time: Should I return to Wales?

The chart said no. Not a resounding: No. But, on balance, best not. Spotting the New Moon – an ill omen in Horary - conjunct the Descendant of Dorothy's Death Chart, I decided to stay put. Although I missed my mother, I didn't want to move so far away from Bill; nor did I want to leave Dorothy's grave unattended; her story as yet unearthed. So, during my next school holiday, the February Half Term, I brought out my certificates and looked at them again.

Dorothy's father been retired out of the Police Force and had died aged thirty-five when she was nine years' old. Had she blamed herself for his death, I wondered, as children often do? Her mother had remarried in 1916 and been widowed again. That can't have been easy either. Still, I imagined Dorothy would have coped: her occupation of private secretary (at the time of her marriage) suggested a responsible, organised person; good in a crisis. Not that there would have been many careers open to a woman of her background in those days as I knew from my mother's case. Had Dorothy, like my mother, longed to go to University only to find family finances wouldn't allow? But when details of her will arrived in the post (via Martin, the Friendly Librarian) it seemed that her material circumstances had not been as modest as I had supposed. She had bequeathed the sum of eight hundred pounds, no small achievement in 1946, to her husband, Wilfrid. He, some ten years later, had bequeathed his estate to one Edith Priscilla Pook, widow.

'His comfort,' said Bill, 'in his old age.'

'No children then.'

'Doesn't look like it.'

'Poor Dorothy.'

'And poor Wilfrid.'

I began stacking the dishes. 'I wonder why she didn't leave anything to Peter.'

He shrugged as he topped up his wine. 'Who knows? She may have met him after she made her will. She may have made her will upon marriage and never changed it. Or maybe he didn't want anything from her.'

'Oh, yes.' I brightened, remembering the inscription. 'It's 'to you, the stars, narcissi fields and music.' And people weren't as materialistic in those days. I expect Wilfrid met Edith after Dorothy died. What do you think?'

'I have no idea.'

'Only it struck me, supposing Dorothy doesn't know? Could this be what she wants me to find out?'

'You want to find out.'

'Well, of course I do. But maybe that was it. Wilfrid was having an affair and Dorothy didn't know but had her suspicions.'

'If she was anything like you she did. Poor old Wilfrid, that's all I can say. I imagine he never got a moment's peace. Of course, what you're forgetting is that Dorothy was the one with the lover.'

'Oh, we don't know that at all. We don't know who Peter was.'

'And we don't know who Edith was either.'

'Hmm. I suppose there's an outside chance she may have been their daughter, wouldn't you say so? If she had married very young and been widowed, say, in the Second World War?'

'Unlikely. I think you'll find she was his comfort.'

'Oh, I hope there was a bit more to it than that!'

'It's not to be sniffed at, comfort,' he replied. 'It's no mean thing.'

So, who was Edith, I began to wonder; and I stewed on it for a while; but then I let it drop. I was too busy to go off in search of Edith or anyone else. My mother had a spell in hospital at the beginning of March, and then I was busy spring cleaning. I wanted my house to look good because I was going to open it up during Art Weeks. I had started painting again during the previous winter. I'd painted portraits, the view from my living room, my cats asleep on the chair. In the spring, the daffodil bulbs I had planted on Dorothy's grave blossomed on cue. I had my narcissi fields. In May, Bill had a daughter - born under the sign of Taurus.

VENUS PHOSPHORUS

July 11th 2000.

The best part of a year had passed since Bill had met Madeleine; and now, on Dorothy's anniversary, a dream of my own was coming true: Bill and I were attending Evensong in a local chapel.

It was a small and compact chapel; the congregation equally small - just me, Bill and the vicar, who appeared nervous and embarrassed which may have had something to do with the fact that Bill subjected him to a sardonic smile and penetrating gaze throughout the rather brief service. The theme of the service was, 'Letting Go of the Past,' which seemed appropriate under the circumstances: we had asked for a blessing on our forthcoming marriage. However, the reading, from the Old Testament, contained a fair amount of smiting and blasting of crops, which had rather less of a romantic ring. Still, Bill loved the irony and we burst out laughing as soon as we got outside. I can't remember what we sang. Again, just me, Bill and the vicar. It may have been, 'Nearer my God to Thee.'

Afterwards, we walked home through the churchyard and I laid a couple of the pink carnations Bill had given me on Dorothy's grave. And it was while we stood there chatting that he suddenly announced, and without any prompting from me, that he had been talking things over with a friend, and they had decided that since my illnesses were psychosomatic, my health would improve after we got married.

'But what if it doesn't?' I said, plummeting rather rapidly from Cloud Nine.

'It will,' he replied. 'Therefore, the sooner the better.'

I looked down at my bandaged feet and began to worry. Supposing it didn't improve, supposing it got worse? What then? After all, when he'd asked me to marry him, he'd called me his Rock; <u>his</u> Peter - not his Wreck.

'Aren't we rather rushing into things a bit,' I suggested over supper.

'Oh yes, after all we hardly know each other.'

'No, I only meant, I'm beginning to feel perhaps we don't have to do it by the end of the month. It makes me feel pressured.'

'There's no reason for you to feel that way.'

'But that is how I feel, Bill. I've got Venus in Taurus, I don't like to feel rushed, and I need to be sure you've sorted your finances before we get married. I've got Eleanor to consider, not just myself.'

'You're putting conditions on it. You don't trust me. I've told you I'll sort things out at my end and I will. You concentrate on what you have to do.'

My task was to book the Registry Office. We had also agreed that I would choose an auspicious day. As luck would have it, however, an auspicious day and the Registry Office were not available at the same time. Furthermore, at the end of the week, Venus was involved in an eclipse.'

'This isn't a good omen,' I told Bill.

'For you.'

'It doesn't augur well for either of us. And you can hardly expect me, an astrologer, to get married when Venus is involved in an eclipse. This would be like expecting a Catholic to get married at Stonehenge.'

'So what about all these other happy couples, I wonder - the ones who got up early enough in the morning to book the Registry Office - are they doomed?'

'I don't know about them,' I replied. 'It's the chart for the moment you proposed to me I'm looking at. The Lunar Eclipse falls on the position of Venus in that chart. Oh, but hang on, Bill, what are you talking about? I did get up early in the morning. I told you the 'phone was engaged. By the time I got through, somebody else had booked the last slot. They pipped me at the post - the other couple. They slipped in: Venus eclipsed.'

He reached for his glass of wine. 'You've changed your mind.'

'We just have to wait for a better time. Let's have another think when we're on holiday, we can't do anything before then anyway.'

The following day, I drove down to visit my mother – 'though not to discuss wedding plans.

'You look dreadful,' she said as I walked through the door, 'I hope nobody saw you come in.'

'Don't worry, I used the tradesman's entrance.'

'You did not.'

'All right, I didn't.'

'You may think me a nag, but I do wish you would wash your hair.'

'I can't, my eczema's flared up again.'

'You don't look after yourself,' she complained, 'I can't imagine how I brought you up to be so casual about your health.'

'You didn't.' I began rummaging in my bag. 'Now, where did I put your new slippers?'

'No, I didn't that's for sure. If you'd seen the things I've seen, you'd appreciate the Gift of Life. Oh, but why do I bother. You never listen to me. Where's Eleanor?'

'I must have left them in the car.'

'Where's Eleanor?'

'Out with Alison and the Girls, they've gone to the beach. There's some kind of carnival on. I'll bring her in tomorrow morning on our way back.'

'Please do. So, you'll be breaking up from school soon?'

'Yes, thank God. I can't wait for the end of term. I'll be able to get on with my research.'

'I'll believe that when I see it.'

'Now, Mum, that's hardly fair. I've just marked over a hundred A' Level papers.'

'You haven't been marking A' Level papers since March.'

'No, I've been marking Coursework.'

'You've allowed Bill to distract you again.'

'Well, I do have a life, you know. Or, I wouldn't mind having one.'

'You've got a very easy life, compared to the one I had.'

'All right, Mum. Could I not have a lecture today, do you think? I'm very tired.'

'Yes, because you don't look after yourself. You don't eat properly and you don't keep sensible hours. You behave like an adolescent. Your daughter, who is an adolescent, is a lot more sensible than you. I'm telling you, Gwendolen, you're your own worst enemy. Self-destructive, like your father. Well, you've made your own bed and you are going to have to lie in it now. I can't help you anymore. I'm no use to you anymore. No use to anyone.'

'Oh, Mum, don't talk like that.' I moved towards her but took a step back when she waved for me to keep my distance.

'I'm sorry to find you so low,' I added, 'I know it's awful for you, stuck in that chair.'

'Oh well, and I'm sorry I'm so ratty, I can't help it.'

'You're frustrated. It's a nightmare for you. I'd hate it. I do understand.'

'Yes, that's the trouble with you. You make excuses for everybody - hopeless.' And she turned her head away.

'I'm going for a walk,' I said, 'I'll come back after you've had your nap.'

'Just as you like.'

When I returned, I found her in a much better mood. She'd been on her Nebulizer and got a bit more air into her lungs. We sat for a while looking through photographs, then went through her funeral arrangements again which she seemed to enjoy; nodding like an old-fashioned school teacher listening to a pupil recite the content of a lesson she had been required to learn off by heart. And, of course, just to keep me on my toes, she occasionally changed the content. A few weeks back, she had wanted flowers; now she had decided against them. In April, she had wanted a male voice choir; now absolutely not. A year ago, she had wanted a woodland burial; now, the public cemetery. She remained consistent, however, in her wish to avoid cremation (because it would upset Eleanor) and in her absolute determination that neither Church nor Chapel should be involved.

'You have got that, I hope.'

'Yes, yes.'

'Good - because I'm not having you sneaking God in by the back door. I've warned your brother. Watch out for your sister, I said, she'll try to sneak Him in when she thinks I'm not looking.'

I smiled. 'Oh, yes, you'll be keeping an eye out for me, that's for sure. It wouldn't surprise me if you hired a private detective. But you know, there's no way I'd go against your wishes, Mum - although I can't pretend I'm happy with them. I feel uneasy.'

'I'm sorry you feel that way but there's nothing I can do.'

'You could tell me why.'

'I have told you. You don't listen. Because it would be hypocritical. I'm not a Christian, neither was your father, and neither are you.'

'Oh, Dad believed in God, I think.'

'He believed in Albert Gaskell.'

'Heaven is on Earth, he used to say, and Hell is in No Man's Land. He may have been a Buddhist.'

'There weren't any Buddhists in Barnsley when he was growing up. But never mind your father, it's me we're talking about here and I'm not having religion at my funeral.'

'Oh, I blame your grandmother.'

'My grandmother? What did she ever do to you? You didn't even meet her.'

'She was a Bible-thumper; and she gave you poisoned sweets.'

'Oh, you're exaggerating, as usual.'

'You were very poor. It was just after the First World War. You'd never had any sweets, and your grandmother gave you poisoned ones. She came back from the shops with a bag of boiled sweets and dipped them in something nasty which made you very sick.'

'Ah, yes, so she did. Cascara and Bitter Aloes. Well, fancy you remembering that. So, you do listen to me sometimes.'

'I listen to you a lot, Mum, actually. Yes, I've often wondered why she did it. I've often thought it may have had something to do with her religion - all that hell fire and damnation stuff: We are all born in sin and must be punished - even when we haven't done anything wrong.'

'But we had done wrong. We took the sweets.'

'No, Mum; she set you up. She told you not to eat them, but she knew you were watching when she hid them: you and Uncle Emrhys, hiding behind the long, thick, crimson velvet drapes.'

'That's right, we were. Yes, I can see her now, her long black skirts and the old Welsh dresser. And the look on her face when she found us – triumphant!'

'What a terrible thing to do.'

'It wasn't very pleasant, I admit. But I doubt it had anything to do with her religion.'

'I think that could well have been the reason.'

'No, there doesn't always have to be a reason. I saw enough of it during the War, believe you me. They'll hang a small child because they don't like the look of her mother. Now, you'll tell me it was because of religion or their childhood, or they've been brainwashed. You make excuses, Gwendolen, because it makes you feel better. But it's better to wise up and look it squarely in the face. My grandmother? She had a streak of the same. It was in her nature. Nothing to do with Original Sin.'

I nodded: I'd heard her speak this way before. 'The thing is though, Mum, there could be another kind of God, couldn't there, who doesn't give children tests they can't pass. Other religions have different Gods.'

'They do,' she replied, 'And I'm not having any of them at my funeral either. No, your task is to read the King's Broadcast at the Outbreak of War, and keep God out of it.'

This perplexed me: 'I don't see how I could do that. It wouldn't make any sense.'

'God isn't in the Broadcast.'

'Yes, He is.' And I quoted the relevant passage.

'Hmm, that doesn't sound quite accurate to me.'

'Well, I got it from your diary.'

'All right then, if that's what it says in my diary, we'll go along with it. I do want the King's Broadcast because it moved me at the time.'

'I expect it gave you hope.'

'No, I don't recall feeling hopeful at the outbreak of War, I must say. Not with Matron handing out cyanide pills in case of German paratroopers. I want the King's Broadcast because it moved me, and those were the most important years of my life. They made me who I am.'

'All right, Mum, never fear, you shall have it. Your wish is my command.' And I waved an imaginary wand.

'Oh, you've always been a fairy, and now you're my fairy godmother. Well, you can magic yourself into the bathroom and wash your hair.'

'I can't, I told you, my hands.'

'In that case, go back to your brother's and get Alison to wash it for you. Go on, before they arrive with my afternoon tea.'

'So how did you find her today?' My brother asked, as we sat on his terrace over-looking the sea.

'Hmm? Oh, very low when I arrived; perked up during her funeral plans; then got frantic just as I was leaving, telling the girl who brought her tea how hopeless I am. But she didn't keep it up for quite as long.'

He nodded thoughtfully then opened a can of beer. 'She's not going to change now, Gwen, let's face it. That would be too much to expect. Still, she's not doing too badly, is she? The last report from the doctor was very encouraging, I thought. And did you notice, she's been trying to write with her left hand? How's that for determination. She'll never give up, will she, our Mum. She'll outlive you if you're not careful.'

'Did you want me to hang round for supper, Dan, or shall I walk off now while the tide's in?'

He gave a gently ironic smile, reminiscent of my father. 'Now, you know I didn't mean it to come out that way, but I am worried about you. I had hoped that with Mum down here, and more settled, your skin would have started to clear up. But if anything it's looking worse.'

'Bill says it's psychosomatic. It could well be.'

'And what did the specialist say?'

'They're not really sure. Apparently it's common in women of a certain age who smoke. There could be a hormonal component.'

'Perhaps you should stop smoking.'

'Oh, don't you start. I've got enough people telling me what to do.'

'Okay, I'm sorry. That wasn't fair. So, maybe what you need's a change of scene. I know money's tight, but I'd be happy to fund you.'

'That's really good of you, Dan, but I'd rather feel I could turn to you in an emergency. I'd rather you'd help me out then.'

'You don't think this is an emergency?'

'No. Anyway, I'm going away for a week with Bill. His sister's rented a cottage and invited us to join her party.'

'That was good of her.' He took another sip of his beer. 'And when you get back – what then?'

'Sorry?'

'You've postponed your wedding plans, I take it. Only you haven't mentioned them.'

'Oh. No, I've postponed them for now. The Registry Office is booked until September.'

'Hmm, well, if I were you I'd postpone them indefinitely. I didn't want to say anything before because you were so full of it, but I've talked it over with Alison and we don't think it would work. You like to be your own boss, and so does Bill. And it's always been a bit of a roller-coaster ride, hasn't it? And, I don't know, maybe you like it better that way, the pair of you, so why change it? I'm surprised, actually, that he asked you to marry him after all this time. What do you think brought it on?'

I laughed. 'You make it sound as though he had an attack of something unpleasant.'

'No, I was just wondering why now? It's not as if anything's changed, is it? You're no different, he's no different. The only thing that's changed is that he's now got a child which is a big change, of course.'

I began to feel uncomfortable, 'I know that, Dan, but she doesn't live with him.'

'She doesn't live with him yet.'

'She lives with her mother and I should think she'll continue to live with her mother.'

'I daresay she will, but anything can happen in life. No, you need to think this through very carefully, Gwen. Would you really want to be cast in the step-mother role? And how would you feel about the child under the circumstances?'

'I'm over it,' I said, reaching for my cigarettes. 'Really, I'm not upset about the baby, Dan. She was meant to be.'

'You think you're over it, and maybe you are; but you won't mind me giving you a bit of brotherly advice, I hope. I say to keep things as they are. It wouldn't be fair on Bill, either, for you to marry him then find you couldn't hack it; and it wouldn't be fair on Eleanor. Well, that's my opinion for what it's worth, and I'm sure that's what Dad would have said. At least don't make a decision until your health improves.'

I nodded and looked out across the sea – would it ever improve?

By now I was heartily sick of this eczema, it was slowing me down during the day and waking me up at night. I did stop smoking for a while and tried various natural remedies but the eczema refused to budge. I read somewhere that it can be caused by repressed anger so I bought a cheap chair and tried bashing it with a rolling pin. The chair collapsed, the eczema remained. Oh, well, I told myself, as I ironed Bill's clothes ready for our holiday, no one ever died of eczema – although I might die of exhaustion at this rate. Where was he? We were meant to be leaving at the crack of dawn and it had now gone ten o'clock.

Shortly before midnight, the 'phone rang. His friend, Louise, had 'broken down' during dinner so he would be staying until her housemate returned home. He couldn't leave her because she had a 'history' (the nature of which, he did not, divulge).

Well, I thought, as I sat in the garden on his smoking bench, this is one of the things I like about him, of course, his concern for his friends, but do I really need to marry him since he already treats me as a wife? But before I could get any further with that train of thought, he arrived with a bunch of flowers from a garage, then proceeded to give me a break down of our itinerary while I cleaned out the thermos flask.

On my way to bed, I glanced in the landing mirror. I looked tired and drawn. Two red splodges had appeared on my cheekbones as if a toddler had been playing at make-up, and my eyes looked more grey than blue. Maybe I should take Dan up on his offer. I really could do with some time out when I could shut myself away without responsibility for anyone one else. Now, I don't recall offering this thought to the Cosmos as a prayer, but I did have occasion before much longer to contemplate the meaning of the old saw: be careful what you wish for.

Towards the end of our holiday, Bill cooked a chicken concoction; and as I watched him, I began to feel uneasy. He was performing like a television chef: a glass of wine in one hand, a spatula in the other, and peppering the conversation with witty remarks. Anxiously, I looked around the circle, but no one else appeared concerned so I told myself I was being neurotic and ate some. I won't bore you with the details. No one else ended up in hospital. I got worse on the journey home.

Bill cleaned up my kitchen as we waited for the doctor to arrive. Was he turning into my mother? 'I can't believe you've allowed your kitchen to get into such a state. When was the last time you cleaned behind the stove?'

Was I turning into my mother? 'I can't go into hospital, Doctor Robbins, they don't clean as well as they used to - I might catch something else.'

Was Eleanor turning into me? 'I know you can't eat but I've brought you some wine gums. You like wine gums, I know.'

My mother, thankfully, remained true to herself. She got her carer to send me a nightdress as she felt sure I would not possess a suitable garment.

A few days later, I checked myself out. I hadn't fully recovered, but, after spotting some blood in the communal lavatory, I decided I'd be better off at home. Tucked up safely in my own bed, and in my own nightdress, I began to make plans. I was determined to celebrate Dorothy's forthcoming birthday: she would be one hundred years old.

MARS

August 6th 2000

On Dorothy's 100th birthday, I met a Martian. A young man, strong and fit, approached me while I stood at her graveside; and a very belligerent young man - or so it appeared - for without concern for a formal introduction, he launched into a veritable tirade against the Church authorities for allowing the graveyard to deteriorate so badly.

'Well, yes,' I said, when I managed to get a word in, 'I feel quite strongly about it myself.'

'I know you do,' he replied, fixing me with an intense look. 'I've seen you down here before. But what do they care, eh?' And he shook his fist at the church before gesturing towards a small colony of war graves partially obscured in the undergrowth some distance away. 'Bloody bishops, and priests and politicians, can't even keep their graves clean when they gave their all.'

'Yes, it's not very good,' I agreed, 'but the Army did come down earlier this year to do some clearing up.'

'Doesn't look like it to me.'

'No, well, it's grown back a bit since. It's a nightmare, actually, getting rid of nettles. But they were here, burning off the undergrowth around the war graves. I think they were a pioneer regiment.'

'How do you know that?'

'Lily told me. You may have seen her? She comes down every day to feed the churchyard cats.'

'I know. Game old bird. Look of a sparrow hawk. She's got respect. Same as you.'

'Well, I hope I have,' I replied. 'I try to visit the war graves when I can. Mainly on Remembrance Day. My mother likes me to. She was a nurse with the Eighth Army - and afterwards, in Europe. My father fought in the War as well.'

'You don't look old enough.'

'Oh, thank you very much, that's very kind of you to say so. No, I was born after the War. My father died of his wounds later, which is why he's got a war grave.'

He nodded towards the war graves. 'One of those, is he?'

'No, he's buried in Brighton. He was a St.Dunstaner. They've got a plot in the cemetery for men and women blinded on active service.'

'Oh, blinded was he? That's bad.'

'Yes, a machine gun bullet ricocheted off a post.'

'He wouldn't have known that would he?'

'No, he always thought it must have been blast. But my brother and I went over there for the D-day Commemoration, and met the Sergeant who was with him at the time. They were fighting for a village called Annebault. He was in a ditch, on the walkie-talkie, radioing back their position.'

'So what did he do, raise his head?'

'Something like that. They were on the advance and hadn't had any sleep. I expect he lost concentration. He was only twenty.'

'Brave bloke.'

'Yes, very. He lost his sense of taste as well. But there you go. It was a job, he said, it had to be done and that was all there was to it.'

Again, he gave a short, sharp nod. He tended to punctuate his speech with these, I noticed, or by pulling harder on his hand-rolled cigarette. 'You come down here a lot,' he said. 'You come for some peace and quiet, I know. I do.'

And that was when he told me about his son. Or, rather, told Dorothy. Moving closer towards the grave, he maintained a steady gaze upon the headstone while speaking more softly of his son. He had a son, he said, who had died in infancy and was buried somewhere else. But where his son was buried, it was immaculate. They did look after the graves. They kept the hedges trimmed, the grass perfectly clipped; and there were proper gravel pathways, all fully-lined so the weeds didn't poke through. Where his son was, it was all above board, exactly as it should be - nothing to complain about there.

'I'm sorry,' I said. 'It's terrible when a child dies.'

"S'all right,' he replied, abruptly shrugging it off.

'So you and I have both got someone – somewhere else.'

'Yep. So, what about her then, Dorothy - she family?'

'No, no. I just like to visit her grave. I sort of adopted it ages ago.'

'And Peter? Was he her husband?'

'I don't know. Her husband was named Wilfrid.'

'Could have been her name for him.'

'Yes, I did think that at one point. When I found out he was a Capricorn, I thought he may he have been her Rock, but then I thought, probably not.'

'You're into that, are you, Astrology? I'm not.'

'No? Well, it's not everybody's thing.'

'Not going to tell you you're wrong though.'

'Oh, good,' I replied. 'That'll make a change.'

He almost smiled.

'So, what do you make of the inscription?' I asked.

'It's okay. Grave's in a bit of a state though.'

'Oh, yes. I'm sorry. I normally keep it up but I haven't been well recently.'

'What's wrong with you?'

'Eczema, and I got food poisoning, but I'm all right now.'

'Not a hundred per cent though.'

'Well, no.'

'Hmm. Tell you what, I'm a stonemason by trade. Or was. I could probably do something about the subsidence.'

'Could you?' I hesitated at the idea of Dorothy being disturbed. 'You'd have to dig quite deep, wouldn't you?'

'No, no. She'd be okay.'

'Are you sure?'

'Yep, no problem.'

He then proceeded to tell me how he would go about it, in very precise detail. He would dig so far down, insert a plinth and apply a chemical to kill off the algae. Bleach wouldn't do it. He had a stronger chemical back home in his yard.

'Well, I have been worrying about the inscription vanishing,' I said.

'No need.'

'I'll pay you, of course.'

'Just for the materials. It won't take long. An afternoon's work.'

'You must let me pay you for your labour.'

'No,' he repeated, beginning to sound angry again.

'Perhaps I could get you something then - something to drink, or tobacco?'

'If you like.'

'So, how will I contact you?'

'You'll come down here - by this time next week - and you'll see that it's been done. And when you see that it's been done, that's when you call me.'

As he left, I realised I hadn't got his name or address; although I did have his mobile number and I had asked him for his date of birth. I hurriedly scribbled the details in my notebook then returned to Dorothy's grave.

'Well, what do you make of that?' I said. 'There I was feeling sorry for myself, and asking you to give *me* a present on your birthday and send me Peter; and it turns out you're going to get a present after all.'

And smiling happily, I too, left the churchyard in something of a hurry, anxious to relay this news to Bill. With any luck, I would catch him in the local café where he liked to do his morning crossword. Sure enough, there he was, dug-in to his usual booth.

'You'll never guess what just happened to me in the churchyard,' I began, but before I could get much further, the Stonemason himself walked in; acknowledging me with a nod, and Bill with a thumbs-up sign.

'Do you know him?' I asked, incredulous. 'Because that's the man I just met in the churchyard who offered to restore Dorothy's headstone.'

'His name is Kiwi,' he replied, returning to his crossword.

'Kiwi? Isn't that a fruit?'

'It is, yes.'

'So, how do you know him?'

'I met him through Madeleine. He's a friend of hers.'

I felt my heart sink. 'Oh.'

'Yes, don't worry. You can trust him.'

'Do you think so?'

'Yes, he is perfectly trustworthy. Comes from an army background.'

'Really?'

He filled in another clue. 'So I was told.'

'It's an odd name, though, Kiwi, even for a nickname.'

'Not if you were born in New Zealand. His real name is Peter.'

'What!' I nearly shot out of my seat.

'Thought you'd like that one.'

Now, this really was too much. I'd asked Dorothy to send me Peter and I'd got an ex-army friend of Bill's twin. This did not bode well. This boded very far from well. Would he do it?

When I got home, I went straight to my Ephemeris. He had the Sun conjunct Mars, conjunct Saturn – rather an apt signature for a stonemason. He had the necessary skills. Oh, and it was improving. His Moon in Aries conjoined my Sun. No wonder I had warmed to him. Even better, he had the Lunar Node in exactly the same degree as Dorothy's Venus - and my father's. He had sympathised with my father and wanted to beautify Dorothy's headstone. He had wanted to, but would he get round to it? Like Dorothy, he lacked the Element of Earth. But then he had a strong Saturn, he might. The chart for the moment I met him would reveal more.

It revealed – more Neptune. Oh, no, would you believe it: there he was again, the old Sea God. Oh, wasn't it just my luck. Even worse, Mars was opposing Neptune at the Nadir. Was he about to venture overseas? Or drown his sorrows in some other dismal place? His motives, I felt sure, were honourable: Mars in the proud sign of Leo. He had given his word. He would want to fulfil it, but Neptune intervenes; dissolves and confuses. Something - or someone would get in the way.

'If anything gets in the way,' said Bill, calling round after lunch, 'it'll be you monitoring him.'

'I'm not monitoring him, I've only just met him.'

'But you will be, if I'm any judge. Will he, won't he? You'll be worrying it to death. Just leave it alone and it will happen.'

But the chart turned out right. He didn't do it that summer, and he hasn't done it yet. Dorothy continues to subside as the elements do their work; the inscription slowly fading: Neptune at the point of the grave.

'So, what was all that about?' I asked Dorothy when I returned from my week in Wales to find he hadn't made a start on the work. 'I asked you to send me Peter and you sent the Stonemason Who Never Was. Was that your idea of a joke? Well, I don't think it's funny, Dorothy, because I'm all in now, and I really could have done with some help, and what did I get? A fruit, a fruit named Peter!'

Which was when I heard her. Or thought I did. Oh, who knows what I heard. But it was a voice and it didn't sound like mine. For a start, it was much too calm.

So, Peter was not the man you thought he was.

This felt odd, unnerving. But I stood my ground and stamped my foot.

'Is that it?' I demanded.

No response.

'Now, listen here Dorothy, I know Peter isn't the man I thought he was; I'm not a complete idiot. I know very well that he isn't a stonemason from an army background who goes round offering to relieve people of their subsidence; I have grasped that much thank you. So will you please stop messing about and send me the Real One next time. Why? What do you mean, why? Because I want Peter, that's what I want!'

And I stamped my foot again. But I was running out of steam, and by the time I got home, I was pouring with sweat. I took a bath, but it didn't really cool me down.

'Perhaps I should give up,' I told Bill over dinner. 'Maybe this strange business with the Stonemason means there is no Peter, it's all been illusion, and I'm wasting my time.'

He shrugged, 'Maybe you are. You're looking for something that doesn't exist, that's for sure. And it's not all it's cracked up to be, either, Romance, I can promise you that.'

'I don't know what I'm looking for.'

'Aren't you? I thought you were looking for Peter.'

'Yes, but I'm not sure what Peter represents.'

He shrugged then reached for his wine glass, 'Peter is Kiwi.'

'No he isn't. Peter is not the man I thought he was.'

'That was your own voice telling you what you already knew.'

'Yes, I suppose. Oh, I don't know, Bill, I'm tempted to give up. I haven't been well. And yet it is such a bizarre coincidence.'

'That's exactly what it is, a coincidence.'

'Yes, but there has to be more to it. I mean, you reach a point where you think, this is a coincidence too far. Well, I feel I've reached that point.'

'You notice these coincidences when other people would ignore them,' he replied, 'because you are especially alert to them. And you are especially intuitive because of your childhood. You had to be. We've been here before. Of course, when you notice something there's a message in it, I'm not denying that, but it's a message from self to self. So, what was it about this coincidence? How do you feel about it?'

'I think I'm baffled.'

'Not think, feel.'

'I'm not sure. Disappointed, I suppose.'

'Well, there you are then, that's your answer. You noticed this coincidence because you expect always to be disappointed. That's what you're like.'

'But I was hoping he would do it.'

'Yes, you are ever hopeful. That's your first response. But below the surface, you expect to be disappointed, so you notice those experiences, the ones which disappoint.'

'I often do feel disappointed,' I agreed.

'Yes, you do.'

'But that's because I often am! Oh, I know what you're getting at, Bill, but it can't be the whole truth. It wouldn't explain all these coincidences. Or why I found Dorothy's grave in the first place.'

'Yes, well, who knows about that? Who knows what you were doing in the churchyard that day. You can't even remember. But you must have been feeling something.'

'Empty,' I said, 'I do remember that because I was filled up.'

'You felt filled up.'

'No, I was filled up. And then there was the extraordinary coincidence of Dorothy's death. Well, that wasn't just a coincidence.'

'Yes, it was.' 'So why do you think I found her grave, and not the grave of, say, Mary Buggins who died of 'flu'?'

'All right,' he said, topping up his wine glass. 'Do you really want to look at this again?'

'Yes. It might help me sort things out.'

'Very well, we will. There could be a number of explanations. There may have been something in the colour, the shape or texture of the grave, which appealed to your senses. But it's more likely that the inscription appealed to your Romanticism. It struck a chord for you. Or it could have been tribal. You were born in Wales. Your mother is Welsh. So you zoomed in on the word, 'Taffy.' Then again, there could have been a spy satellite setting you up by beaming thoughts directly into your head. Or a mystic gas emanating from Dorothy's grave. Or a natural gas. The latter, the Gas Hypothesis, at least, would be checkable.'

'You believe in things which can be checked?'

'Not at all. I don't <u>believe</u> in them. But they do have a virtue. You can find out whether they are right or not. They're the interesting ones. They get a tick or not.'

'And what if you can't find out?'

'Then it's idle speculation of course. There are things for which there are no explanations: coincidences, for example. How you take them is a matter of personal choice. But it's character or temperament that determines how you take them, not some hidden factor explaining how they happen. There's nothing extra in the coincidence itself. Coincidence is neutral. I take that as a point of logic.'

And with that, he returned to his book of Bridge Moves while I went into my cupboard under the stairs and brought out the chart for my meeting with the Stonemason.

There was something in what Bill had said about disappointment, I felt sure, and I could see it in the chart. I could see it in the connection between this chart and my Birth Chart, for I was born with Neptune in exactly the same place, at the Nadir; where we begin and end. Also the place of the Father.

Had I been disappointed in my father? Surely not. My father had been a hero and I exalted him to any passer-by who would lend an ear. Oh, but wasn't this what I'd been doing when I met the Stonemason - the Stonemason who was not entirely as he appeared? I began to feel uneasy and wiped the sweat from the back of my neck. Oh, but I had exalted my father, I wasn't disappointed in him. So that was all right then. It wasn't possible; I simply couldn't imagine feeling anything but love for a man who'd been battered half to death on a battlefield. And if he drank too much, that wasn't his fault. Of course he needed to put himself out. He'd had countless operations on his head. How he suffered while he blamed no one and never complained. And if he gave up in the end, how could I blame him for that? No, I was never disappointed in my father; I missed him. I missed him terribly. *I have every confidence in you*, he always said. He had been my champion and I was his 'Little Eyes.' So that was all right then. Except I was still sweating.

I passed my hand across my forehead, which felt clammy and hot. There <u>was</u> something in this coincidence, if only I could see. Did it have something to do with birthdays? It had been Dorothy's birthday but I had asked her for a present for myself. Was there something in that? Bill said I couldn't accept presents, was that true? Sometimes I did, sometimes I didn't. Did my father remember my birthday? No. But then he didn't remember his own. Did Bill remember my birthday? No. And was any of this remotely relevant to anything at all?

I looked up at Bill, still engrossed in his book. He was very perceptive but there was one thing he could not explain to my satisfaction; not through logic, nor psychology; which was this: why do all these strange things keep happening on Dorothy's and not my father's grave? Why her? Why Dorothy Browning? And why Peter? There <u>was</u> a connection between Dorothy and Peter; between Bill, my father, the Stonemason and myself. If only I could see. And I tried: I tried very hard to fit the pieces together. But it was no good; I couldn't see beyond this; and, worse, I had now given myself a splitting headache.

'I'm off to bed,' I told Bill, 'I've finished in the kitchen. Will you do the lights?'

'Uhuh,' he nodded, still lost in his book.

That night I had a terrifying dream. I was in hospital, in a corridor on a trolley. The door of an operating theatre loomed into view. The Stonemason was the surgeon. Or was he the anaesthetist? He was wearing a mask and a gown but I recognised him at once. The window in the door was blacked-out. There were scalpels and knives. There was a canister of gas. I felt sick. I was terrified. Then it went dark.

Then I was somewhere else. A different dream? A different scene. Except this also involved an operation. Richard, my astrological penfriend was inserting matchsticks under my eyelids to keep them open. He was willing me to see, I could feel it and was doing my utmost to resist. Then the Stonemason was back again. This time carving an epitaph on a marble floor while my father flew over his head. He looked happy. He was bathed in a golden light. But he was still blind. My eyes filled with tears; and then I awoke. I was burning up.

'Is it any wonder you get ill,' said Bill, slapping a strip thermometer onto my forehead.

'You're not well and you keep going down to the churchyard. Carry on like this, and you'll be joining her only it won't be your ovary this time, it'll be pneumonia.'

'You were probably delirious,' said Eleanor, topping up my glass of squash in the morning. 'These bugs take a long time to work their way out of your system, Nana says. You're to drink lots of fluids, stay indoors and take Paracetamol four times a day.'

'She rang, did she?'

'Yes. So did Jo. And Richard's coming when he gets back from his holiday.'

'Ah, so that's why I dreamed about him.'

'It was just a nightmare, Mum.'

'No, he and I go back a long way.'

She smiled, and plumped up my pillow. 'Now, you're always telling me you don't believe in Reincarnation.'

'I'm not inclined to - but Richard does.'

In my imagination, Richard had lived in the South of France during the Middle Ages; an impression I'd formed on holiday when I came across his exact likeness inscribed in a plaque on the wall of a hotel called, 'Les Templiers.' Needless to say, it turned out to be someone from a completely different era, a writer and artist named

D'escossy, but he was Richard's double all right: same sharp features, strong jaw-bone and deep-set eyes. Rather austere, he always wore a black duffle coat: in one pocket, his Midnight Ephemeris; in the other, various homeopathic remedies which he distributed freely to ailing friends.

'It's really good of you,' I said when I met him from his train: 'What is it?'

'Aurum,' he replied, delving into a small brown paper bag. 'Gold. It'll strengthen you. The Sulphur is for your skin, the Nat Mur for your other symptoms. And there's a Blackthorn tonic. You shouldn't have come out, you know, Gwen, I could have got a taxi.'

'Oh, Richard,' I said, taking his arm, 'you've come all this way.'

On our way home, we stopped for coffee in the covered market; spent a pleasant afternoon looking at charts; then he and Bill argued fiercely about the Nature of Reality over tea.

'The trouble with Richard,' said Bill, as he left for his game of Bridge, 'is that he's got to be right. He has to win. He's on a crusade.'

'Oh, well, he is an Aries.'

'I haven't got the measure of Bill yet,' said Richard as we waited for his train. 'He has a brilliant mind but he doubts everything. You and he argue a lot, don't you?'

'You know me, I love a good argument.'

'But not about anything personal.'

'Not really.'

'So, mainly about ideas?'

'By and large, yes. What are you getting at?'

'I'm not sure. I shall have to give it some thought and get back to you. Your Mars opposes Saturn doesn't it?'

'That's right. Same as Dorothy.'

'Hmm, well, that's not easy of course. And where was Mars when you fell ill? Remind me.'

'Square my Neptune in Scorpio. Well, that's the beauty of Astrology, isn't it: I might be under the weather but at least I can console myself with symbolic fittingness.'

'It is rather apt. Mars squares your Neptune in Scorpio and you are invaded by a poisonous bug. But you know, Gwen, this didn't happen the last time Mars was there. You let yourself get very run down. Now, that wasn't your fault. You were up against it, what with your mother and everything. But you do need, now, to conserve your energy and build yourself up. If you'll take my advice, you won't be in any hurry to return to school. Ask the doctor to sign you off for a couple of weeks. And keep away from arguments. I'll have another think, as I said, and get back to you.'

'You'll keep me posted,' I said.

'I will.'

Before he could do so, however, Bill and I were arguing again. Only this time, it was about something personal. During the last week of August, and without prior notice, Madeleine arrived to spend a holiday in Oxford - and under his roof.

Couldn't she stay with friends? I asked. Why did she have to stay in his house? Because, he explained, he needed to rebuild. He needed to get to know his child therefore he needed to reassure her mother. This all sounded perfectly reasonable and I agreed with him. Yet, by the end of the week, I had worked myself up into a fever of grief and rage. It didn't console me in the least to think that Bill had my interests at heart when he told me not to call round during her visit. Nor did the certain knowledge that he no longer desired Madeleine alleviate my pain. Nothing could ease it. Nothing. Not after the day I ventured out and saw her with the baby: for it had now become real; their dream, fleshed out. They might not be together, but they were united in a way that he and I could never be: in their hope for the future, a beautiful baby girl; dark-haired, well-made, solid; the image of the man I loved. It stopped me in my tracks, this image, and I broke down where I stood. It was too late for me now; I was all done in, barren. But my pain was full of life. It pulsed and heaved inside me; hot, wet, bloody and full of life; twisting and turning in monstrous parody of the child which may once have been, but which would not now be, ever. Turning into the churchyard, I leaned against the wall and wept. I was still weeping when Bill telephoned from a callbox later that night.

He couldn't understand it: what on earth had got into me? I was hurting myself, and guilt-tripping him, and he wasn't having it.

'I'm not hurting myself,' I wailed, 'I'm just hurting, hurting, hurting -'

No. He remained firm and calm: I was hurting myself and guilt-tripping him. And I could choose not to. I could try trusting.

'And you could try feeling,' I sobbed. 'You could try feeling sympathy. You felt sorry for your twin. Try feeling sympathy for someone who's not like you.'

A controlled sigh. He would reiterate his main point. I could choose not to hurt myself. And, really, my illness was no excuse. He had cured himself of his illness.

That did it. That stopped my tears - just like that.

'Well done,' I yelled, 'Oh, well done, Bill, aren't you clever.'

And so another ending: rebellious Mars opposing ice cold Uranus across the horizon. And yes, not a kind word was said on either side.

MERCURY

I resume this narrative with a confession: I began writing it before Bill's daughter was born and he knew that I was writing it. I recall reading him various drafts of the opening chapters while he made a number of suggestions as to how I might improve the text. Nothing major, the odd word here and there; a grammatical error I needed to correct. Generally, I found his advice quite helpful 'though I was less than enthralled by the ending he came up with during one of these late night discussions. The narrator, he suggested, should somehow discover the exact date and time she first found Dorothy's grave so that she could cast the chart for this seminal moment which had so far eluded her grasp. Now, how might this happen?

She could undergo hypnosis. But, no, this might unearth more than she bargained for. Better for her to meet someone in the churchyard who had been present on the day in question - and who still remembered her, even after all this time – because her eccentric behaviour, while standing on the grave, had struck him as profoundly weird and disturbing. Now, who might this be? An ex-Army man, perhaps. Someone who spent a lot of time in the churchyard himself. An obsessive-compulsive type, like her mother. He would have watched as she stood on the grave, then returned forthwith to his Spartan bed-sit in order to record the event in the diary he always maintained, true to his training, with faultless precision. She would thereby receive the exact time and date for the moment of discovering the grave and could ponder the chart until it yielded a satisfactory answer.

'I like it,' I said, 'that is, I like the idea of the chart turning up after all this time. That would round things off rather nicely. Trouble is, it's not very likely to happen, is it?'

'It's a story; you make them up.'

'It isn't a story; it's what's happening. I'm writing it as I go along.'

'It's still a story - your version of events. In a story, you invent.'

'But I can't invent a horoscope.'

'Of course you can. You astrologers do it all the time. What do you do when you cast a chart to choose an auspicious moment for, I don't know - opening a new cat flap.'

I smiled, 'Oh, I know, Bill, but this is different because it's already happened. I can't go back in time and invent a chart. I'm sorry, I just don't fancy tinkering about with the cosmos in that way. No, much as I like your ending, I'm afraid I shall have to find the Real Peter.'

'Oh, well,' he replied, leaning back in his chair and lighting-up. 'That's easily done. You do know, I take it, that 'Peter' and 'Taffy' are colloquialisms for the male member.'

'Oh, don't be ridiculous. That's the most ridiculous thing I've ever heard. They are not.'

'Yes, they are. It's common knowledge. They are both another word for cock.'

'Well, I've never heard of it, and I hardly think a woman of Dorothy's calibre would have a penis on her headstone once never mind twice. No, really, Bill, you're winding me up.'

'Am I? Very well, we'll see. We'll get a dictionary.'

But as he moved to get up, I waved at him not to bother, 'I don't care whether it is in the dictionary, I'm not having a penis on my headstone and that's all there is to it. You'll have to do better than that.'

'All right then,' he said, sighing deeply, 'I'll try again. Tut, some people are never satisfied.' And he placed his hand across his brow. 'Ah, yes, I have him now. There he goes: whoosh, Peter, tackling an S.S. Panzer Division single-handed armed only with his battered copy of the Penguin book of Romantic Verse. Oh, but hang on, something's going wrong. Oh, no, he's been captured by the Gestapo. Will he manage to extricate himself before they get the thumbscrews out? Not without Divine Intervention. Ah, but not to worry, it duly comes. He escapes from the Gestapo and wins the Military Cross - awarded for services to King, Country and innumerable W.A.A.Fs: - one of whom he marries after his sight is miraculously restored while she sits praying for him in a bombed out Belgian church.'

I nodded. 'Very good, Bill. Yes, very droll. But where does Dorothy fit in? She wasn't a W.A.A.F.'

'Dorothy is the moralist who persuades him he is one of God's Chosen when she hears of his miraculous escapades whereupon he resolves to abjure all pleasures of the flesh in favour of the priesthood. There, you've got it. Peter was her priest.'

'I'll try it on,' I said, 'I'll try it on and see what people think.'

So, that's what I did: after our 'bust up,' and to help take my mind off things, I put the Priest Idea before the Court of Public Opinion.

My friend, Karen from school (who'd brought a basket of fruit, and a little light reading from my Head of Department entitled, 'Coursework Strays,') thought it, 'a pretty crap idea.'

'No,' she said, settling down into the armchair and pulling her knees up; 'he doesn't half talk a lot of bollocks, Bill. He was winding you up - because you wouldn't marry him, I expect.'

'Oh, I think he probably just got carried away with his wit.'

'Hmm. Not a very nice thing to say 'though, was it - about the war-blinded soldier in a bombed out church? I'd have had his balls in my frying pan.'

'Yes, well, you have got a very strong Mars in your Horoscope.'

'Have I?'

'Yes, in Aries, opposite Pluto in the House of Nether Regions.'

'Yep, that'd explain a lot.' Reaching into the basket, she pulled a black grape and popped it into her mouth. 'So, what's going on with them then - is that Madeleine still in his house?'

'As far as I know. But never mind them. What about Peter?'

'Who?'

'To you, the stars, narcissi, fields and music - Peter. Who do you think he was?'

'I've got no idea.'

'Oh come, on, K, tell me a story.'

'I'm not a storyteller, I teach P.E.'

'Everyone's a storyteller. Come on.'

'Oh, go on then since it's you.' Pulling another grape, she spat the pip into her hand. 'Okay. He was her friend - not her lover - because there's nothing possessive in the inscription. He really loved her, wishing her well, so they never had sex - that would be my guess.'

I laughed. 'So, he could have been her priest.'

'No, I reckon they were lifelong friends. They may have been childhood sweethearts. Yes, how about this? He went off to the trenches, came back at the end of the War, and found she'd married someone else, thinking he'd been killed. But he didn't blame her, and they always stayed friends.'

'Oh, that's really sad,' said Eleanor, peering over her magazine. 'Can't we have a happy ending? Can't we have Peter coming back from the War and bumping Wilfrid off?'

'What, a murderer, you mean? Well, that's certainly a far cry from a priest.'

'I don't really think he was a murderer, Mum, but he definitely wasn't a priest. It's not the sort of language a priest would use. Miss Taylor's right. Bill was just winding you up.'

My sister-in-law wasn't too keen on the Priest Idea either, and came up with an alternative when I visited towards the end of the week. Peter, she suggested, could be the stalker who had been visiting Dorothy's grave, and, since I needed an ending, couldn't Dorothy intervene to save our narrator from some suitably gruesome fate?

'There ought to be a denouement,' she said. 'And we need to meet Dorothy in the flesh.'

'Do we?' I wasn't sure whether I was up to that, but Alison was adamant.

'Yes, we do, we're intrigued by her. After all this time, we want to meet her, and it has to be in the flesh. So, here's a possibility. Someone - as we know - has been visiting Dorothy's grave and leaving strange little offerings for our narrator to find: roses in jam jars, bottles of pop and a musical box. Someone has been hiding in the undergrowth, and becoming increasingly obsessed. He knows there's a man in her life because he overhears her confiding in Dorothy.

Now, one day, he overhears her say something which drives him over the edge. How could she prefer this philosopher to me, he thinks. He doesn't care for her as I do. I've been leaving her all these offerings and watching her every move, but she doesn't even notice. And, in the end, he can stand it no longer. He resolves to finish it once and for all; finish them both off. So, he goes down to the churchyard and lies in wait.

And this is where Dorothy comes in. And this is the twist in the tale. It turns out Peter wasn't her lover but her stalker. He'd been stalking her during the Blackout. So she intervenes to save our narrator from suffering the same fate. She saves you from a fate worse than death.'

'I should think so too, after all I've done for her.' Laughing, I turned to my brother. 'What do you think, Dan?'

'What do I think?' He looked up from his newspaper. 'I think you're both mad. But if you want my opinion, Peter doesn't exist and it's a typical female fantasy. She probably commissioned the headstone herself and got one of her wacky women friends to make sure it was done. Only the friend - being arty and impractical - got the date wrong, while poor old Wilfrid footed the bill and didn't even get a mention. Either that or Wilfrid and Peter are one and the same; and it was her name for her husband.'

'That's what the Stonemason said.'

'Yes? Well, he's probably right – whoever he is. But I know you won't be happy with that one. It's not tragic enough for you. So if I were you I'd stick with the Priest Idea only get him to top himself having lost - not only Dorothy - but his God in the same fell moment.'

'Oh,' I said. 'Oh. Ah.'

'There, what did I say,' he grinned from ear to ear. 'I knew you'd like that one. Mum would like that one too so why not get on with it instead of talking about it nineteen to the dozen?'

So, I put it to my mother when I visited later that afternoon: 'Dan thinks you wouldn't mind if Peter turned out to be Dorothy's priest who was so overcome with grief when she died that he killed himself.'

'Oh, does he? Is that what he thinks? Well, I cannot agree with that. She wasn't a Catholic, was she?'

'Not as far as I know.'

'Of course he wasn't her priest. Really, I'm surprised at your brother.'

'It wasn't his idea,' I said, 'Oh, never mind. Would you like me to make you another cup of tea? I brought you some custard creams.'

'Not for now, thank you. I want to get to the bottom of it. Whatever gave you the idea that Peter was her priest?'

'Nothing. He wasn't. I'm just trying to get people to tell me what they think.'

'No, you mustn't do that. I want to know who he was. Never mind making things up, that's always been your problem.'

'Yes, all right, Mum, I'm not really planning to make him up. But for now, let's have some fun. If you had a choice and he could be anyone, anyone in the world, who would he be?'

And then it hit me - as she turned her head away.

'Oh, God, I'm sorry, Mum. That was really tactless.'

There than came a long pause.

'Actually, would you like me – I've got a bit more time now - would you like me to look him up? See if I can find out whether he's still alive?'

She didn't reply straightaway but looked out of the window across the sea.

'No, it's too late now,' she said after a while. 'But thank you.'

'You'll be reunited,' I said, 'I'm sure you will. In fact, I know it.'

'You don't know that, Gwendolen. Not if you're honest. But it was a nice thought.' She then resumed her normal manner: 'Now don't start on at me about God and Spiritualism or you'll have to go home. All right, we'll have that cup of tea and get organised, I want to make an inventory.'

'But we made one last time I was here, and the time before, and the time before that!'

'Yes, and I want to make another one because there have been thefts. Eleanor will do it for me, won't you dear? I expect *she's* remembered to bring a notebook and pen.'

'Yes, Nana,' she replied patiently, reaching into her bag.

So off we went yet again. We had to unpack all her drawers, write everything down and pack them up again in exactly the same order. We had to bring all her clothes out of the wardrobe, read her the labels out loud, and hang them up again in exactly the same place.

'Happy now?'

'Yes, thank you.' She tilted her head for me to kiss her cheek. I then left her alone with Eleanor so they could say goodbye properly. She could never take affection from me but she could from Eleanor.

'So what did happen to Jimmy?' Eleanor asked as we descended in the lift. 'He wasn't killed in the War, was he?'

'No.'

'So why did you tell me she lost him in the War?'

'Because she did - sort of. She broke it off.'

'But why? She really loved him. There's that photo of her on the beach with him looking carefree and so pretty. She's still got his letters. She's got one in her bag. She's been reading it. Do you know what it says?'

I nodded. 'Not Goodbye, Please.'

'Oh, Mum, Why? Why did she do it? Why did she end it when she loved him, and he loved her so much?'

'Because he was married - and had a child.'

'A married man? I suppose he may have been, but why are you asking me?' Richard sounded very tired as he often did on the telephone these days. Every so often his voice would crack through sheer exhaustion - or it could have been exasperation. 'You always ask me what I think, Gwen, but it's for you to find out. You have a Mercury

Karma. Mercury conjunct the Node. Now, isn't Mercury about to turn direct in your Progressed Horoscope?'

'I'm not sure. It's probably going retrograde, knowing my luck. But can we forget about Karma for the moment, Richard, and you tell me a story?'

'Oh, I don't know about that; that's your department. But all right then, if you insist. Remind me of the inscription again.'

'To you the stars, narcissi fields and music. Peter.'

'All right: he was an astrologer - the stars. With Leo Ascendant – narcissi fields. And Venus in Taurus - love of music. Ah, does that sound like anyone you know?'

I laughed, 'I should think he was probably her friend.'

'It seems quite likely. But you'll find out.'

Still smiling, I rang Joanna, catching her just as she was about to put her feet up after cooking the evening meal and emptying the dishwasher.

'I don't know, Gwen, it's tempting to think he was her lover; but it still bothers me that he got the date wrong. Then again, we know how forgetful men are when it comes to anniversaries. Do they attach the same importance to these things as we do? Or is it because we women have always done it, so they have never had to learn? Of course Eleanor wouldn't make a mistake on your headstone. But Dorothy didn't have a daughter, did she?'

'No, she didn't have children.'

'I suppose he could have been another family member then. Something similar happened to me once, actually, when my grandfather died. The family put one of my poems on his headstone – and my name - which felt a bit peculiar, seeing my name on a headstone when I'm not dead.'

'I should think it did,' I replied, 'Yes, that must have felt very odd. So, you think Peter was a family member, do you?'

'He could be. But, of course, it's really a mystery.'

We then drifted away from Dorothy and Peter and into the saga of my love life – which meant that by the time I finally put the 'phone down, it was definitely too late to ring anyone else - with the possible exception of the Samaritans.

Ah, now that was an idea. Could Peter have been a Good Samaritan? I did actually have a friend named Peter who lived in the North of England, volunteered with the Samaritans and had visited Dorothy's grave on one of his rare trips to Oxford. His only response, however, to the question I had sent him by letter, was that he hadn't the faintest idea who Peter was but would I please let him know when I found out. Meanwhile, could I pass on his regards to Dorothy? This I duly did, calling in for a chat on my way to the post box, and bumping into Lily, opening a can of Felix for the churchyard cats.

'She's had three visitors this week,' she said. 'And how are you getting along?'

I shrugged, 'Oh, all right. Not too bad.'

'Well, you go and tell Dorothy all about it. She'll understand, I'm sure. Well, I believe it, don't you? You go and talk to them and they do listen, and they do reply, though not always in ways you'd expect.'

'Yes, well, I enjoy our little chats, as you know. It always helps to get things off your chest. But these three visitors, Lily, did you notice whether one of them was a man: an army type, good-looking but a bit under the weather? Or tall, dark and lean, more of a swarthy type?'

'Oh, no, I don't think so. There was a man, but he looked more like a schoolteacher to me: old-fashioned, with a short-back-and sides and a duffle coat. Came on his rickety bike, and parked it against a tree. Then there was an old girl walking her dog. She stopped and had a bit of a think. And a younger woman, about your age, in a woolly hat. Looked to me like she had a bad cold. But I didn't see any army types, no. But they do say the Army's coming back again soon. She'll like that, won't she? It'll be a lot easier to get to her grave. But until they do, I'll keep Michael on the look-out. I know he's a drinker, but he's as good as gold.'

'He's probably a Leo as well,' I said. 'This patch, round here, is becoming a bit of a Leo stomping ground.'

'Oh, I don't know about his star sign. I hadn't thought of that. I'll ask him. But, now, don't you worry. He'll keep an eye on things and so will I. We'll let you know if she gets any more visitors.'

'Well, Dorothy, it seems that you're acquiring quite a fan club,' I said. 'I don't know how popular you were in life, but you're certainly popular now. In fact, I'd say you were becoming something of a socialite. Anyway, my friend Peter has sent you a post card - with a Tigger on the front. And here it is. Now, what do you make of that?

What do you mean, I know some strange men? I can assure you that Peter is perfectly normal. In fact, he's a lawyer. Ah, now, could there be a message in that? Yes. Could he have been the lawyer you consulted when you were contemplating divorce? Wilfrid was a totally selfish chauvinist who kept you chained to the kitchen sink and kept picking holes in your character. You didn't cook enough potatoes. You didn't look after his needs. Your kitchen was a right tip. And everything was always your fault even when you got ill. So you were saving up your housekeeping on the quiet and planning your get-away?

Oh, but I'm just going round and round in circles now, aren't I. I've got so many different versions of Peter, I honestly think I'm losing the plot. So, it's over to you again, Dot: - lover, lawyer, stalker, friend – who was he?'

Pondering this question well into the small hours that night, I felt a prompt and drew up a Horary Chart. And the answer? Saturn in Gemini: the writing on the stone. Damn, Foiled again. No short cuts for me then. Nevertheless, I decided to present the chart at the next meeting of Mercury Phosphorus, a Divinatory Astrology group which met in those days in the farmhouse residence of its founding member, Evelyn Harrington, an astute Gemini with old soul eyes, short white hair, and old soul Capricorn rising.

'It's interesting that your Ascending Degree is rising,' she said, projecting the chart onto her screen, as cake and biscuits did the rounds.

I reached for a chocolate digestive. 'I hope that doesn't mean I'm him.'

'No, no. You are the Querent. Leo rises so you are signified by the Sun. And here you are in Virgo, writing and doing lots of research. And you have been rather bothered by your health, unfortunately.'

'Ah, but what about Mars?' Her companion, Moira, who was knitting a scarf in exactly the same shade of orangey- red as her hair, leaned forward and jabbed her needle in the direction of the screen. 'That's a very potent Mars you've got there, Gwendolen, in the First House.'

'I haven't got any Mars in my house at the moment,' I replied.

'Neither have I - more's the pity.' Scorpio, Cassie, put in.

'Nope, me neither.' Annie dunked a shortbread in her tea and gave a plaintive mew as it dissolved.

Oblivious to these comments, Moira resumed her thread. 'I still think that Mars has got to be telling us something. It'll have something to do with the War, I should think. Or the Stonemason. I can't help thinking it's highly significant, Gwendolen, that strange dream you had about the operation. I wouldn't be surprised if you heard from him again, and quite soon.'

'Hmm, he could still do it, I suppose,' I replied. 'But what about the Neptune factor?'

She shrugged. 'It just won't be what you expect.'

'Yes, that's right.' Annie wiped biscuit crumbs from her cheesecloth smock. 'With Uranus in the Seventh, you're in for another shock.'

'Thanks very much.'

At this point, Daphne, who'd been dozing in the fireside armchair chair (an elderly tabby in her ample lap) woke up. 'Where's the Moon?' She called out. 'Twelfth house? Asylum, Hospitals, Retreat from the World. Does that sound like you?'

'We're not looking for Gwendolen this evening, Daphne,' said Evelyn. 'We're looking for Peter who is symbolised by Saturn, Lord of the Seventh, in Gemini, in the turned Fourth House.'

'Dead,' we all agreed.

'He is also in the Tenth House of the Radix,' she continued. 'I'm inclined to favour the turned chart in third party questions, but we might consider the Radix since we've ruled her father out.'

'Her mother?' said Annie, bemused.

'An authority figure, 'said Evelyn. 'Her employer, or someone she met during the course of her career.'

'I'm not sure she had a career after marriage,' I said. 'Apart from being the Wife of Wilfrid.'

'Ah, but Saturn rules the Seventh,' said Cassie. 'Perhaps it's Bill.'

'Very funny,' I said.

'And weren't you engaged to a Capricorn once?'

Since this wasn't strictly astrologically accurate, I decided not to reply.

'I still think we should be looking at the Moon,' said Daphne. 'The conjunction with Neptune in the turned Twelfth suggests the anaesthetist, who may have slipped up. He may even have had a drug problem. A lot of them do, you know.'

'Yes, I'm not sure we should take the Twelfth as unfortunate,' said Evelyn. 'Retreat from the World can mean many things. Dorothy may have met Peter on an actual retreat. Was she religious, Gwendolen, do you know?'

'I've taken it for granted she was spiritual,' I replied. 'But would the Moon signify Peter really? I'm not convinced. Saturn seems the most likely candidate to me; and in Gemini, a writer, or teacher - something to do with communication.'

'You will hear something I'm sure,' said Evelyn.

'But will I find Peter? Am I, the Sun, in aspect to Saturn? Doesn't look like it.'

'You didn't ask that question.'

'Maybe I should.'

But there weren't any takers.

Looking at the chart again now, I find the Moon's location in the House of Retreat rather apt because I spent the second week of my convalescence contacting matrons of old folk's homes throughout the region. I was trying to find an elderly parishioner who might remember her, but, alas, the Moon's conjunction with Neptune only presaged more confusion. Most of the old folk had become somewhat senile, and those who remained alert had no recollection of either Dorothy or Peter although they loved the inscription (as did a number of their care attendants).

My mother, however, was not impressed.

'You're wasting your time with these old biddies,' she boomed down her telephone. 'You can take it from me, you'll get nowhere with them, I know what they're like. No, what you need is a plan of action. Have you made a plan? I don't suppose you have. Well, go and get a pen and I'll tell you what to put in it. You don't have to follow it to the letter, but it will give you some idea. You need to find a living relative.'

So, thanks to my mother, I bumped into Bill - while sticking a postcard requesting information in the local newsagent's window.

'I wouldn't be too eager to trace a living relative, if I were you,' he said. 'They might not be too keen on the idea of a strange woman rooting around in their family tree. Some might consider it perverse or ghoulish. I wouldn't be too keen on it myself.'

'But you don't bother with your ancestors,' I protested. 'Your grandfather whose memorial I found on my last trip to the Battlefields, whose body was never found ...'

'Yes, yes, you told me. Many times.'

'Well, you've never visited him.'

'No, because he's dead!'

'Well, so is my father but I wouldn't mind if someone visited his grave, or took an interest in him. I'd be pleased, actually, especially if I couldn't manage to get down there myself.'

'Yes, not everyone on this planet's like you. In fact, no one is. I'd tread more carefully, if I were you, in the Land of the Living.'

And with that, he marched off. Still angry, I realised. He did have a point, 'though; and suddenly I felt awful. I felt a dead weight drop straight through me and into the floor. It had never occurred to me that anyone would mind my adopting Dorothy's grave, and that made me feel even worse; the fact that it hadn't occurred to me. *You are the centre of your own little universe,* my mother used to say, *and there's only room in it for one other person and that's your father,* which used to upset me no end. And now I had done it again. So, after this reminder from Bill, I went off the whole idea and dropped it just like that. I stopped badgering elderly parishioners. I stopped writing letters to librarians. I stopped pestering probate officers. I gave up. As a result, my 'phone bill decreased.

Oh, but, hang on, you are saying, looking ahead. You can't have dropped it because we've got at least another three planets to go and possibly an asteroid.

Ah, but how do you know it's me who wrote the rest? How do you know it wasn't my friend Joanna (a novelist) or Eleanor, or my sister-in-law (now trying her hand at radio scripts) or even Dorothy herself, channelling via a medium in the Spiritualist Church. You don't. You'll just have to take my word for it!

URANUS

Of all the bizarre events to have occurred so far during my search, not one of them has shocked me so much as this: a young lad, hurtling through the churchyard as if being chased, stopped abruptly in his tracks a few feet from Dorothy's grave, looked back at me and said, 'Is that your grave?'

And the part I found shocking? I didn't know what to say.

'Er, no, I just look after it,' I managed, just before he sped off, whereupon I waited for the boys I'd assumed to have been chasing him to appear. They didn't. The churchyard was deserted. No sign, even, of Lily, or the churchyard cats. And then I felt the cold. It moved in from the place where he'd stopped in his tracks and politely enquired, 'Is that your grave?'

I began to shiver as it slowly dawned on me that I hadn't thought there was anything unusual about his appearance, yet he had been dressed according to the fashion of my own childhood: hand-knitted grey jumper, short trousers, and tumble-down socks. He could have been my brother, my cousin Gerard, the boy next door.

'If you don't mind, Dorothy, I think I'll go home now.'

'It's probably the onset of your menopause,' said my mother on the telephone. Ever one to look on the bright side, she added: 'Because you've only got one ovary, you can expect the Change of Life early. You can expect hot flushes from now on.'

But I still felt cold. 'The thing is, he wasn't wearing trainers.'

'What's that got to do with anything?'

'And people don't knit jumpers for boys nowadays.'

'Some do, I suppose,' she replied. 'Oh, but I knitted you some lovely woollies when you were a child. Do you remember, Gwendolen? You always looked a treat in lemon. Of course, your hair was always clean and shiny then.'

'I think I'll forget about it now.'

'I would, if I were you.'

So, I did. I pushed the strange boy to the back of my mind, and got on with whatever I was doing at the time. This morning, I woke seeing an image of his face. Not that this surprised me. Yes, something very odd has been happening, I've noticed, since I've been typing up my hand-written drafts on my new computer. Events corresponding with the nature of the planets have been occurring in this establishment in weird and unpredictable ways. When I was typing up Neptune, for example, a

Buddhist called round for a chart reading and left his meditation mat behind. Except I didn't see him arrive with it, I didn't see him leave with it, nor did I see it anywhere in my house. Before it rematerialized - in his temple – he had threatened my Astrology students (whom he suspected of foul play) with 'occult action.' By then, I was typing up Pluto. Ah, well, back to the plot.

After deciding, the day I met Bill outside the newsagent's, to drop the whole thing, I soon changed my mind. I'll do what I like, I thought, as I raked another pile of rubbish from Dorothy's grave into a bin-liner. It's me who looks after it, and if it weren't for me, Dorothy would have disappeared under layers of mouldy fruit, hypodermic needles, broken bottles and pornographic magazines long before now.

This latest one really took the biscuit. I had never seen anything like it in my life, and I sincerely hope I never will again. Fortunately, the worst bits were obscured under layers of congealed curry sauce, but even so, it was an outrage.

'God help him, if I catch him,' I told Dorothy. 'There won't be a lot left of him, by the time I've finished with him. He'll be fertilising your next-door neighbour. Except it wouldn't be fair on her. So, don't worry, I'll restrain myself.'

And with that, I picked up the magazine, and chucked it into a skip full of builders' rubble on my journey home, cackling to myself as I skipped along.

'The little men in white coats will be coming for you before much longer,' said Eleanor as I recounted my exploits with glee.

'I struck a blow,' I said, 'I struck a blow for Feminism.'

'You're beginning to sound like Nana. You'll be telling me next you're not senile yet, and you never get a decent cup of tea. Oh, she rang, by the way, while you were out. She wanted to know whether you'd sent off for the electoral records.'

'I hope you told her I have. '

'Well, I didn't know that, did I? I told her you were in the library.'

'But I'm not in the library.'

'No, but you will be soon, won't you. I've got friends coming round.'

'Oh, that's a shame. I thought you might like to come with me.'

'No, thanks, it's boring.'

'Boring? But, Eleanor, you enjoy research.'

'No, I don't.'

'Yes you do. You got a very good report for History. Top of the class.'

'I might be good at History, Mum, but that doesn't mean I enjoy it. In fact, I hate it. And I'm not going to choose it as an option for G.C.S.E.'

This came as a real blow. 'Oh, but, Eleanor, you're the next generation. You have to keep the flame alive – for the sake of the ancestors.'

'No, I've had enough of dead people now. That's your thing, not mine.'

'Oh, you'll change your mind.'

'No, I won't.'

'Yes, you've got plenty of time before you have to choose your options.'

'I'm not going to change my mind, Mum, no matter how much pressure you apply. I'm going to do Technology – and Textiles.'

'Technology? Textiles? You can't do those, they're not proper subjects.'

'Er, yes they are.'

'No, no, no: you'll be bored out of your brain. You can't even knit. No, Eleanor, you're not the crafty-type. You're very intelligent but you don't like studying, so you should do History because it's all skills nowadays and no knowledge. You'd sail through the exam.'

'I know that, Mum, but I'm still not doing it for G.C.S.E. And I'm not coming to the library with you either. I told you, I've got friends coming round.'

'Hmm, I could always go another day, I suppose. I don't have to go today.'

'Oh, for God's sake, Mum, stop dithering, you're getting on my nerves. You don't need me to come with you at your age. I know why you want me there: it's because I found Dorothy. You think I've got to be there whenever you make a find like I'm your lucky charm, but you can easily find the next one on your own.'

I reached for my coat. 'You're still my lucky charm even if you don't come anywhere with me ever again. You're my little egg.'

'I'm not,' she replied, 'I'm not an egg. I'll be fourteen in three weeks. Go away.'

So off I went, somewhat upset, it has to be said. Calling in at Tesco, I bought a chocolate éclair, which I ate while selecting a new pen in Honest Stationery. It might bring me good fortune, I thought, since my Lucky Charm had chosen to sit this one out. But when I arrived at the library, I received another blow. Martin, the Friendly Librarian, had been replaced by a young woman who sat, unmoving, in front of a computer screen, which meant I would have to do my research myself.

I was now left with two remaining leads. Dorothy's probable brother, George (mentioned in her mother's will) and Edith Priscilla Pook, the widow to whom Wilfrid had bequeathed his estate. Finding either of these in the records wasn't going to be easy, but since I knew where Edith had lived, I decided to start with her. Without any dates, of course, this was going to be a nightmare. I would have to plough through all the Pooks who had lived and died in the twentieth century and even then I might not find her: she could have emigrated, remarried or changed her name.

'Oh, this is hopeless,' I groaned as I plonked myself down in front of the Microfiche Reader and switched on the screen: 'Oh, where do I begin?'

Which was when I heard it: *1972.*

Turning, I looked over my shoulder. No, no one behind me, and no one sitting next to me either. At a neighbouring table, a couple of students were silently taking notes; and in the comfy chair on my right, an elderly gent had fallen asleep with a copy of the Telegraph folded across his lap.

I took a deep breath. Okay, I thought, it's possible I really am starting to hear voices. I've had a lot to deal with. I've always been highly-strung. I could well be developing a certifiable mental illness. Only one way to find out. What you have to do with voices - put them to the test. So, picking up my notebook, I headed for the Index for 1972, and found Edith Pook straightaway. Not that I reacted with any enthusiasm. Rather, I felt strangely detached.

Her death had been registered in the June Quarter, and since it had occurred after 1969, her date of birth was also given. This meant I wouldn't have to send for her Death Certificate so I could save myself some cash - although I should probably send away for Wilfrid's since I hadn't done so yet. Returning to the Index once again (since I'd forgotten when he died) I found the record, hurriedly copied down the details, then returned home to cast the chart for the moment I'd heard *'1972.'*

At first, I wasn't sure how to judge this chart since I didn't feel that I had necessarily been the one who had made contact. I would not, therefore, take the planet ruling the Sign on the Ascendant to signify myself, but would break with tradition and look at it differently.

Once again, the fateful South Node of the Moon was rising (as when Eleanor had found Dorothy in the parish register) suggesting a voice from the past, but which one? Opening my Ephemeris for the date of Edith's birth, I couldn't find any planets connecting with this chart, although I did note that her Sun, in Aquarius, was very close to Bill's. Meanwhile, the Moon applied to the opposition of Pluto. So, more news of the dead then, I thought, assuming that this had not been - as Bill would have said - 'a message from self to self,' and I braced myself for a further shock. And, as always, the Cosmos obliged.

A few days later, Wilfrid's Death Certificate arrived, revealing his change of direction. No longer an artist, he had been employed as a security guard at Her Majesty's Treasury at the time of his death, which had been registered by Edith Priscilla Pook, of the same London address.

'His comfort,' Bill had said, 'his comfort in his old age.'

Some comfort, I thought - for during his time with her, he had ceased being an artist. She wasn't going to support him while he painted: she was no Dorothy. No, he could go out and get himself a proper job. Even worse, she had had him cremated. Why hadn't she buried him with his lawful wedded wife?

I didn't like it. I didn't like it one bit; and was still brooding over my charts when Annie called round on her way back from her yoga class. 'Well, poor old Edith,' she said, perching on the edge of the sofa and kicking off her pumps.

'What do you mean, poor Edith?' I replied. 'She wouldn't let him paint. And she had him cremated.'

'Oh, come on, Gwen. It's hardly likely she'd have had him cremated against his wishes; and as for his painting, anything might have happened. He might have been in a car crash or something; lost the use of his arm.'

'In which case he'd have been no use as a security guard – a one-armed security guard sitting on the nation's gold bullion, I don't think so.'

'All right then, if he stopped painting, it was his choice. Or he could have had a breakdown after Dorothy died, or become depressed. That's more like it. Have you looked at the Astrology? What did he have going on when Dorothy died?'

'Pluto opposing his Moon, and Saturn opposing his Sun.'

'Well, there you go then. Something put out his lights.'

'Yes, yes, but we have free will. The planets are signs, not causes. He didn't have to go underground.'

'Okay, so maybe he felt like a change of scene? People do that. They can have more lives than one. You've done it often enough. Look at all the different things you do with your time.'

'Yes, but it's hardly an improvement - from artist to security guard.'

'Stop being such a snob!'

'Well, it's not - not for a painter. A painter needs light and air, not to be cooped up in some dismal basement. It wasn't for the money. They weren't poor. So why did he do it?'

'I've got no idea, but when you think about it, it's very sad - for all of them. He lost his Dorothy, his inspiration, maybe? Then along came Edith and picked up the pieces. So, sad for her too. All she got was the pieces.'

'I hadn't thought of it that way,' I said after a while.

'No.'

'I've been jumping to conclusions again.'

'What, you? Never.'

'It suppose it makes sense.'

'She was a widow, I expect she understood.'

'Perhaps she was his housekeeper.'

'Would it matter if she wasn't?' Opening her carpet bag, she brought out a bottle of mineral water. 'I don't know, Gwen - strikes me you need to be careful not to project your stuff onto them, especially when you're in this frame of mind. You're not angry with Edith, you're angry with Bill.'

'I'm not angry with him anymore,' I replied. 'I never hold onto anger for long. I'm an Aries.'

'Well even so, leave Edith alone. She did you a favour in the library, I'd say. I should think she was a really nice woman.'

'I'm sure she was,' I replied. 'Of course, we don't know that it was Edith in the library.'

'Who else could it have been?'

'No idea.'

'Was it a woman's voice?'

'No, it was neutral. It didn't have any particular character. Well, it didn't say much!'

'Hmm, it is very odd.' She took a sip of water. 'I know you're not sure about Reincarnation, but it must have crossed your mind, surely, at some point in all of this, that you could be a reincarnation of Dorothy?'

'Well, I do talk to myself when I go to her grave.'

'No, I'm being serious. There are so many connections between you.'

'No, it doesn't add up for me, Annie, and I really don't like the idea of Reincarnation.'

'Just because you don't like it doesn't mean it's not true.'

'Yes, but when you consider the way we behave, and what we're doing to the planet, there's hasn't been a lot of progress. We're as careless now as we've always been. And when you consider the moral calibre of people who lead charmed lives, are they really reaping their karmic rewards? If they did so well in previous lives, how come they're not better people, morally, in this one?'

'Okay, fair point,' she replied. 'But it's more complex, I think. I always think of Karma as habit - not you reap what you sow.'

'Yes? Well, I still think it isn't fair. It's hard enough trying to make amends for what you've got wrong in this life, never mind one you can't remember. No, it's just another dogma, Annie. People should make up their own minds and not believe in any dogma.'

'Isn't that dogmatic?'

'No, it's the only way to live. You can't have other people telling you what to believe because then you really are in Hell. And, of course, it's the only way I can bear it - what happened to my father - knowing he suffered in a good cause, fighting totalitarianism.'

'Yes, but how can we be sure our cause is good? Is there ever a just war?'

'That one was.'

'But some people chose not to fight, not to kill. Can you say they were wrong?'

'Yes. They were wrong.'

'How can you say that if you think people should think for themselves?'

'Because you don't stop men like Hitler by turning the other cheek and appealing to their inner qualities, you stop them with a bullet or a knife, and you owe it to humanity to do that.'

'So, what if Dorothy turns out to have been a pacifist?'

'I'll never speak to her again.'

Funnily enough, it didn't once occur to me during my search for Dorothy to think she had ever been anything other than a sterling patriot, prepared to make enormous sacrifices in her personal life for the greater good while valiantly battling the forces of darkness in the Blackout. I imagined her digging for victory; I imagined her driving ambulances; I imagined her offering shelter to bombed-out victims of the Blitz. I did not imagine her attending meetings of pacifists in the church hall, buying goods on the black market, or entertaining Peter in some secret love nest while the sirens wailed. Indeed, I could not imagine, when details of the Electoral Register arrived from Richmond Library, how Dorothy could have summoned up the energy to carry on an affair at all - unless Peter was the care-attendant.

There are no electoral records for the War Years, but in May 1945, Dorothy had her elderly mother living with her. And Wilfrid's elderly father too. Still, at least she didn't have to cater for any lodgers.

Peter wasn't her lodger, or a displaced person, or a bombed-out victim of the Blitz. He wasn't there. And neither was Wilfrid. He returned to live with Dorothy in October 1945. So, where was Wilfrid - too old, at 53 - for military service when he wasn't dwelling in the marital home? He could have been in hospital, I supposed, but then surely Dorothy would have put his name down on the registration form. Could he have been engaged in War work?

The historian I spoke to at the Imperial War Museum didn't think so. 'Careless Talk Costs Lives?' Not one of Wilfrid's.

'Thank you,' I said, putting the 'phone down, by now ice cold.

So, Dorothy was looking after her mother. Wilfrid was not at home. He returned in October. By this time, she would have been seriously ill. Was it guilt, remorse or duty, I wondered, that brought him home in time for her to die?

Taking a deep breath, I reached for the telephone.

'I should think she knew very well where her husband was,' said Richard, 'and in all likelihood, it is perfectly innocent. You don't know where Wilfrid was when he wasn't with Dorothy, but you do know where Bill was when he wasn't with you. That ought to be enough knowledge!

There's a very real danger, you know, Gwen, of the dead alienating us from life. Now, you have always lived in stories. You have a Mercury Karma. So, it's all very well what you're doing with your writing and so on, but keep it in perspective. Don't become obsessed by it. Do other things. Go out more and socialise. You don't know, yet, what it means, but you will find out.'

'Yes, but what will I find out? It's beginning to really unnerve me now, the way Dorothy's life seems to mirror my own. It's not fun anymore. Why do you think that is?'

'You know I can't answer that question for you.'

'Yes, but I'd like to hear what you think. You believe in Reincarnation.'

'I do, and you don't.'

'But I would still like to hear what you think.'

'All right, but remember this is just my opinion. It is possible that you are a reincarnation of Dorothy. There are many parallels, and in the Astrology too. But my feeling is that it's too soon. I could be wrong, but my feeling is that hers was a Life Interrupted.'

'A Life Interrupted?'

'That's my guess. Now, aged seventeen, you were very ill. You nearly died. You had the same operation as Dorothy. Fifty years ago, when surgery was less advanced, no doubt you would have died. And you were born with Neptune at the Nadir - which is anaesthesia. So, you could be a reincarnation. But I'm inclined to doubt it because it's too soon. And yet there is something to explore here because we carry the memory of this kind of injury in our body.'

'Are you saying Dorothy tuned into me because we had a similar wound?'

'Possibly. Her Sun conjoins your Leo Ascendant. It is possible that she observes, relives something through you.'

'You're not saying I'm possessed, I hope.'

'No. Possession is different and very rare. You and she are in the same consciousness, but it isn't ordinary consciousness. You are aware of one another. It's reciprocal. Now, it's pointless trying to analyse and say, what does she want? What must I discover? It's not about that kind of knowledge. You've already done that. You got your History Degree. No, if Dorothy turned out to have, like you: blue eyes, blonde hair and an allotment, what would this prove? The coincidences, the synchronicities maintain your interest. That's the point. So that you do not give up, and you will complete.'

'Yes, yes, but complete what? How can I complete it if I don't know what it is?'

'Stop asking that kind of question. Trust! You are so trusting in some ways. You always have been. But not always in the right way.'

'I trust Dorothy,' I said.

'Yes.'

'And I trust you.'

'Ah, well, you could be making a mistake there. And Bill?'

'Bill,' I said, after a long pause, 'reflects my own scepticism. I argue with him because of my own doubts.'

'Exactly.'

'So, what do you think?' I asked Dorothy. 'I suppose you'd think me a heretic.

Was it a Life Interrupted? I could have cried when he said that, I really could. I don't know why. Oh, I don't know, Dorothy. I don't know what to believe.

When I was a child, I used to think God was dreaming. And I used to worry, what will happen if he wakes up? Then again, I thought it miraculous, because when my father dreamed, he could see. So, I imagine that's why I thought: this is what God does, he dreams us and we come true.

But my father didn't see me in his dreams, Dorothy. Not really. He pretended to. But he only ever dreamed of people he'd already seen.

Oh well, you know me, Dorothy, I've always been a dreamer. I've only got to go to the Battlefields and I'm dreaming it over and over again. I dream about all sorts of people, actually, and most of them I've never met. Which is what bothers me - now I come to think of it - how come I don't dream about you? Because I've met you, Dorothy, haven't I? Of course I have. See you soon.'

It would be stretching the bounds of credibility way too far, I know, to say that it was on this very day that I met the elderly gentleman who would introduce me to someone who may have known Dorothy – so I won't. But it could have been on this day, and it was certainly after the Autumn Equinox that I met Mr Stone in the churchyard. I know because I was bagging up fallen leaves, and there was damp chill in the early evening air.

'That's a terrible cough,' I said, as he approached behind me along the path, wearing a grey gabardine, belted at the waist. 'Are you sure you should be outdoors?'

For a moment, he hesitated, unsure whether to respond to a strange woman on a grave; but then curiosity, or politeness, got the better of his good judgment.

'It is a very chilly evening, yes, indeed.'

'You should be at home, tucked-up by the fire with a good book and a hot toddy.'

'Yes, that would be rather nice. I would enjoy that. But I'm afraid I have business in the church this evening.'

'Couldn't someone else do it?'

'Not really. I'm the Church Warden.'

'Oh? How interesting.'

'I'm not sure that's the word I'd use. This evening, I'm working on our accounts.'

'Well, I hope they've got the heating on in the Church.'

'I shan't know that until I get there.'

'Oh, no, of course. I'm sorry, I must let you get on. But I wonder if I could quickly ask you a question before you do?'

And, being the perfect gentleman, he agreed. Yes, he did know someone who may be able to help me – when she returned from her holiday - a Mrs Verity Hawes, whose connection to the church went back for over fifty years.

'A little before my time here,' he added wryly, handing me her telephone number, before shuffling off, coughing.

'He probably had bronchitis,' said my mother on the telephone. 'And you kept him out in the freezing cold chatting.'

'I didn't pin him to the ground, you know.'

'Bronchitis can be deadly in a man of his age. It can easily turn to pneumonia.'

'Oh, Mum, why go down that route? You should be pleased. He knows someone who knew Dorothy.'

'May have known Dorothy,' she corrected. 'Still, I suppose this old girl may have known someone who can help us.'

'Yes, let's be hopeful, shall we? I've got a good feeling about this.'

'Oh, you and your feelings. Never mind feelings, let's talk practicalities. How long have we got to wait before she gets back?'

Frowning, I reached for my cigarettes. 'I'm not really sure.'

'Not sure? Didn't you ask him?'

'No, sorry, I forgot.'

'Well, go back to the church before he goes home and find out!'

When I got there, however, the Church was in darkness; the graveyard deserted - apart from Lily who was sheltering a couple of drinkers under her golfing umbrella. She gave me a chipper wave which I quickly returned before hurrying off. By now, I was feeling the cold, and also hungry so I decided to go for chips, taking the side gate to avoid the entrance to Bill's road. But alas, my precautions were in vain. Just as I reached the crossroads, I saw him walking towards the bus stop on the opposite side; head bowed, shoulders hunched, and wearing his old brown fleece. Should I call out to him, I wondered. He didn't look too happy. But before I could make up my mind, a car drove too close to the kerb through a dip in the road, splashing me with old rainwater up to my waist. Oh, would you believe it. Wasn't it just my luck?

Ah, but the tide was turning. Within a day or so, I got home from school to find the horoscope I'd ordered from an astrologer in London sitting on my doormat. Wrongly delivered, the students next door had finally seen fit to return it.

'Yes, very interesting,' I thought, mulling it over with my cup of tea. I would have to edit the text, of course; removing all mention of, 'neglecting the needs of the body,' and, 'idealising military men.' But, on the whole, it was very good; very detailed and accurate: my mother would be pleased.

URANIA

Urania is the muse of astrologers; and it is under her auspice that I now include the somewhat abridged version of Dorothy's horoscope which I read to my mother on Sunday the 8th of October during the Planetary Hour of Venus, while holding the text some distance from my face because I'm quite long-sighted and I'd forgotten my specs.

'The picture emerging in this essentially fiery nativity is of an idealistic, generous, and enthusiastic personality; likeable and sociable yet dignified and proud; who will have been challenged to resolve inner conflicts through relationships with others; struggled to concretise her dreams; maintained an optimistic philosophy of life; and been possessed of unusual creative and visionary gifts.

Without knowing her, it is impossible to judge how far she will have managed to bring the fruits of her imagination down to earth. In fact, given the absence of the Earth Element, she may well have lacked the inclination to do so. However, there are certainly signs which indicate that manifesting her ideas will have been difficult: including the predominance of planets in mutable signs, and the alignment between Mars, Saturn and Neptune which, as the closest aspect in the chart, will have been felt most keenly; tempering the Fire, yes, but presenting challenges of its own.

Without house placings, we cannot say precisely how this configuration will have manifested. More than likely, the opposition of Saturn to Mars will have limited the will to action, or caused problems through the repression of anger; while the opposition to Neptune will probably have had an impact on health signifying chronic ailments or illnesses which are difficult to diagnose. The conjunction of Mars with Neptune may have been experienced in her relations with men: on the plus side, a romantic partner possessed of imaginative gifts - even something of a magician: in the worst case scenario, victimhood.

Relationships will also have been also affected by issues within the realm of feeling. Venus in Cancer is the only planet in Water and makes no aspects with the other planets, striking something of a dumb note. Her own feeling nature will have been sympathetic, sensitive and protective of others, yet darker feelings will have been difficult to square with her Leo sense of herself as a noble person and Sagittarian idealism. She may also have projected psychic content onto others given the predominance of opposition aspects.

Having said this, her attractive personality will have ensured for her the benefit of friends and even admirers to whom she could have turned when needing support; and she will also have enjoyed largely positive familial relations.

Her Sun is not afflicted, and the Moon's likely opposition to Pluto can be read as symbolising a powerful mother who will have exerted a strong influence on her daughter's emotional development as a role model.

Probably her greatest strength lay in her powerful intuition, giving her the ability to envisage potentials, see hidden patterns; and enjoy an instantaneous grasp of all the factors in a given situation. This will have afforded some protection against the consequences of her own naivety and the predations of more wily individuals; ameliorating, to a certain extent, the impact of the Mars/Neptune/Saturn configuration mentioned earlier.

With the strong emphasis in Fire (wherein five inner planets are placed) and some access to the element of Air (albeit mainly through the outer planets), she will have enjoyed the benefit of an enquiring mind; taking pleasure in speculation, lively conversation and sharing her ideas. Mars in Gemini affords a sharp wit, and can be verbally combative, but the opposition to Saturn will have reigned this in to some extent. A harmonious trine aspect between Mercury in Leo and Jupiter in his own sign of Sagittarius, will have facilitated access to the Higher Mind, possibly awarding prophetic gifts, while the trine aspect between Uranus and Mercury adds originality to the thought processes: - although when Mercury is Retrograde, there may be something unusual in the method of communication: something not quite direct.

The North Node of the Moon shows where we should make progress in the current incarnation, while the South Node represents qualities brought from previous lives. When Uranus conjoins the Lunar Node in philosophical and questing Sagittarius, the karmic task is to develop an independent belief system; breaking with tradition, bringing something new to the Collective, and moving from superficial knowledge to deeper understanding.

Julian Manly-Hargreaves. September 2000.'

'So, what do you think?' I asked my mother.

She seemed to have been enjoying herself immensely while I read, although the unusually contented expression on her face may have owed more to Eleanor's ministrations than the power of Astrologia to move the soul: she was giving her a facial massage.

'Oh yes, lovely. You'd make a wonderful beautician, dear. Now, if you mix some of that bleaching cream with the pink powder on the tray there, you can do my moustache.'

'No, I think that's your dental powder, Nana.'

'Is it? Oh. Well, just use the cream then.'

'Mum,' I repeated irritably. 'I'd like some feedback. What did you think of it?'

'Hmm, well, now, let me see. I liked the bit about the powerful mother and creative gifts, but I'm afraid a lot of it went way over my head. No, if you'll take my advice, you'll cut out most of the Astrology and keep it simple. You don't want to bore your reader do you?'

'I don't see why not.'

'Now, now, this is just sour grapes isn't it, Eleanor?'

'I don't know, Nana. Would you mind keeping your head still otherwise you're going to wind up with bleached eyebrows.'

'Yes, be careful, Eleanor,' I said, 'or she'll be back in hospital again - this time as a fashion victim.'

At this, my mother gave an exaggerated sigh. 'Ah, if only you would follow my example. After all, you're still relatively young. You don't look after your assets, as your father used to say. Now, look at Eleanor. She's a shining example to you - hair beautifully cut: clothes all matching. You wouldn't catch Eleanor going out with odd socks on.'

I looked down at my feet. Damn, she was right.

'Yes,' she continued, well into her customary stride, 'much as I would like to give you a positive report, I can't, because although you do have a powerful mother, I'm not going to argue with that, I would say I had virtually no influence on you whatsoever. You have always paddled your own canoe. Mind you, I would definitely regard myself as good role model in one crucial respect: I'm a Feminist. There weren't many girls of your generation whose mothers went back to work full-time to pay for their daughter's university education. Your father was dead set against it, if you remember. If it had been left to him, he'd have kept you at home and married you off to one of his paper boys. So, it's thanks to me and not your lucky stars that you're not slaving away over a hot stove right now, and that you've got your independence, because it wouldn't have suited you, Gwendolen, married life, any more than it suited me, you're too independent. You should put that in your horoscope.'

'It's not my horoscope!'

'Yes it is.'

'No, it isn't! It's Dorothy's. Oh, you haven't been listening to a word I've said.'

'Yes, I was. If I've said it once, I've said it a thousand times, I'm not senile yet. I thought it was very good, but it's much too technical. There are far too many technical terms in it: aspects and, what do you call them, nodes. No, no, no; you need to pare it right down.'

'Oh, I give up.'

'Now where are you going?'

'For a cigarette.'

'Ah,' I heard her confide in Eleanor as I left: 'I wish I were still a smoker.'

Outside in the communal garden, I sat down on a bench between two tubs of wilting hydrangeas and lit my cigarette. How on earth could my mother have mistaken Dorothy's horoscope for mine after all my efforts to edit it? I must have removed at least a thousand words, if not more. Oh, she couldn't possibly have thought it was my horoscope. She'd known all along it was Dorothy's; it was her idea of joke. Yes, never mind Dorothy, my mother was turning into a blithe spirit. Either that, or the massage oil had gone to her head, and she had spaced-out on a heady mix of lavender and galbanum essential oil. Ah, now that was an idea. Maybe I should try some myself?

'Miss Gaskell?' A plump girl with pale skin wearing a dark green overall interrupted my reverie.

'Hmm? Oh, yes, that's me.'

'Sorry to interrupt, but Matron asked if you could pop in to her office before you go. I did go up to your mother's room and your daughter said I'd find you here.'

'Oh. Okay. Did she say what it was about?'

'No, she wouldn't have told me that, but it's not urgent – any time before you go.'

Extinguishing my cigarette, I lit another. All right, I thought, if it's not urgent, I don't need to worry. After all, she'd got over her chest infection and was back to her former self. No, more than likely, she'd upset one of the other residents, accused a member of staff of theft, or pressed her buzzer in the middle of the night to alleviate her boredom. Unless my brother was the culprit? Had he fallen behind with the payments; brought his dog inside, soaking wet from the beach; or parked his old Volvo in the spot reserved for the minibus? That wasn't unlikely either. Then again if he had done, surely Matron would have asked to speak to him, not me, to give him the ticking off. Not that she was about to tell me off, of course. I knew that, really. I knew it wasn't going to be great news even before she asked me to make myself comfortable and whether I would like a cup of tea.

'I'm sorry I missed your brother yesterday,' she said, as I perched on the arm of her easy chair. 'I was going to telephone this morning but I knew you were coming today so I thought I would wait. It's always better talk personally rather than on the telephone.'

She then proceeded to give me the latest medical report, which was far too technical. There were far too many terms in it like 'aortic' and 'aneurysm.' No, no, no; it needed to be pared right down.

'The other thing is,' she added at some point, 'she's been in a very good mood lately, less fractious.'

'Has she? That's a good thing, surely.'

'Yes, it's just that - and please, stop me if I'm going too far - there's often a change in our residents when they're getting ready, as if they want you to see their best side.'

'My mother isn't going anywhere,' I said.

'Well, let's hope not yet. But she is reconciled, you know. Have you spoken to her about it? She said something rather lovely to me the other day: 'my life has been a series of journeys, and when I die, I'll be going on another one.' I found that very moving.'

'She doesn't believe that,' I replied. 'She was giving you a lot of flannel.'

'Oh, I got the impression she was being sincere. We were talking about her time in Africa during the War. We had a very nice chat, actually. She brought out her photograph album. She's never done that before. I felt quite honoured. I liked the one of her sitting on a camel in front of the pyramids, I must say. It wasn't all doom and gloom, she told me.'

'No. It was her finest hour.' I glanced out of the window. It looked like a high tide. 'I suppose you've seen a lot of death,' I said after a while.

'I have, and so has your mother. She isn't afraid.'

I felt a lump in my throat. 'No.'

'She's a remarkable woman, really.'

I nodded in agreement, took another sip of tea then brightened. 'Still, it's not as though she's going to die tomorrow, is it? They said it could rupture but they didn't say when.'

'No, they wouldn't be able to say for sure.'

'She could carry on for another year or more.'

'Yes, I'm not sure that's very likely. I could be wrong, but I don't think it's going to be very long now. I wanted to put you in the picture in case you wanted to talk, bearing in mind that she is in a far better mood.'

'I'll think about it,' I said. 'Thank you.'But when I got back, I could see my mother wasn't in the mood for an in-depth talk. She and Eleanor were sitting in the corner, giggling over Dorothy's horoscope and dunking custard creams. For a while, I hovered about, unsure where to place myself, but then she looked up and gave me a knowing smile.

'Now, where did we get to,' she said, 'with *Dorothy's* story?'

JUPITER

My first thought, upon discovering that Dorothy had been a practising Christian, was to go back through this narrative and erase all slurs upon the Church of England - careless clergymen, vacillating vicars, perambulating parish registers - must all go the way of all flesh. But then I thought, no, I should tell the truth; and, anyway, some of them are rather funny. Well, I thought so. And, I decided, Dorothy would have thought so too, for according to Mrs Verity Hawes (whose connection with the Church went back over fifty years) Dorothy 'Taffy' Browning had been, 'rather a colourful character.' She'd have enjoyed a good joke, in other words. In fact, I can almost hear her laughing as I write this.

A colourful character, eh. That surprised you, didn't it? You've been imagining me as something of a martyr, haven't you? Go on. Own up.

No, no, not at all, Dorothy. Really, I'm delighted to hear it. Of course, it's always possible to be a colourful martyr. We don't all wear sack cloth and ashes, nowadays, you know.

By 'colourful' Mrs Hawes had not been referring to Dorothy's sartorial habits.

'She tended to dress conservatively as I recall, although elegant. She was always nicely turned-out, and she always wore a hat. They all did, of course, in those days.'

We were talking on the telephone. At last, she had returned from her holiday and on Wednesday, the 11th of October at 4.16 pm, I had managed to find her at home. I did not, however, cast the chart for this event before I rang since I had the feeling all it would show would be me talking on the telephone to yet another elderly lady.

Mrs Hawes, of course, was no ordinary elderly lady (is there any such thing?). No, she had known Dorothy Browning albeit, 'not very well.'

She had been a child of around nine or ten years of age when she met Dorothy in a house on Magdalen Road run by a community of nuns. Dorothy used to sit with them in their communal living room where they would converse and read aloud to one another. It all sounded very convivial, I thought, listening attentively, and I certainly couldn't imagine Dorothy behaving as I had in childhood: - calling round on the nuns who lived next door to my house in order to regale them with exaggerated accounts of my latest exploits and eat all their cakes. Had Dorothy's nuns baked? I wondered. They certainly sounded a friendly bunch. Mrs Hawes felt sorry that the house no longer existed.

'What happened to it?' I asked.

'Oh, it was closed some time ago,' she replied. 'The nuns have all died, or moved away. But I seem to recall she had some sort of connection with Laleham Abbey, near Staines in Middlesex. But that's closed down now as well, I believe, so that's not much help to you. The nuns - who would have remembered her - are all gone now.'

'They're buried in the churchyard,' I said.

'That's right, they are. Well, how interesting that you found her grave. And you've been looking after it, you said?'

'Yes, I planted the daffodils there.'

'Did you? She'd have liked that, I'm sure. Of course, I didn't know her very well. I was only a child, and it was rather a long time ago.'

'Would this have been during the War, or shortly afterwards?'

'Round about then.'

'After, or before the War?'

'Well now, probably towards the end.'

By that time, I thought, Dorothy would have been quite ill, yet she had managed to impress a young girl with the force of her personality.

'She was a striking person, you know; not so much in her looks as in her presence. She had what I'd call 'presence' if you know what I mean. 'Colourful' is the best way I could describe it.'

'But you can't remember what she looked like?'

'I'm sorry, no. It was rather a long time ago, and she always wore a hat. So, no, I can't remember her face. She wasn't tall, I don't think - but then she was usually sitting down. Ah, but I do remember her voice. She had rather a beautiful speaking voice. Very well-spoken. Cultured. Didn't she write poetry?'

'Did she?' That came as a shock.

'Yes, she was some sort of writer, I believe.'

'Are you sure about that?' I asked. 'She was a private secretary before her marriage.'

'Now, I didn't know that. I always thought she was some sort of writer, and I had thought it was poetry.'

'Perhaps because of the inscription?'

'Hmm, perhaps. Of course, it is very poetic, isn't it, and rather lovely. She was rather a lovely person, really. I've often thought about her when I've walked past. I had thought, perhaps we should earmark her grave as we have done recently with the War graves. What do you think?'

'Oh, yes, that's a very good idea,' I replied. 'I'd love to see the headstone restored so the inscription doesn't vanish. I've often wondered who Peter was.'

'Have you? I've always assumed he was her husband. She was married, I believe, but there were no children. I've always thought that a shame.'

'Yes, she would have made a very good mother,' I said.

'I'm sure.'

'I don't suppose you recall meeting her husband, do you? He was an artist, born in Oxford. I'm quite interested in tracking down some of his paintings.'

'No, I'm sorry, I can't help you there. I didn't know him. As far as I'm aware, she always came to the house alone.'

It had been her sanctuary, I thought, her home from home. 'Well, this has been very helpful, Mrs Hawes, I can't tell you how much this means to me, actually.'

'You're very welcome. If I remember anything else, I'll let you know.'

So, Dorothy Browning — a colourful and cultured Christian: not tall, who visited nuns, may have written poetry and always wore a hat?

'I know exactly the style of hat,' said my mother on the telephone. 'A brown felt one with a short brim. I had one exactly the same when I was demobbed.'

'Aren't you going to congratulate me?'

'No. You haven't finished yet. You've got to find Peter. Anyway, she might not have remembered the right one. I hadn't got Dorothy down as Anglo Catholic.'

But I felt convinced felt that Mrs Hawes had remembered the right person. Without any prompting from me, she had recalled that Dorothy had been married and childless: she had also remembered specific details. Having said this, when I later met her in person, something came up which caused me a few doubts.

I was in the churchyard one afternoon, helping to transcribe inscriptions, when the project leader introduced me to Mrs Hawes. A tall, slender and elegant woman, she didn't say much, just looked at me very intently while I gave her an account of my research.

At last, she spoke: 'Did you say she was forty-five when she died?'

'That's right.'

'Only I had the impression of an older person.'

'No, she was definitely forty-five.'

'Hmm, I definitely had a much older person in mind.'

'Adults often appear older than they are to children, don't they?'

'I suppose so.'

'She may have been ill when you met her,' I added. 'She had ovarian cancer.'

'I suppose that could explain it. I hadn't realised how she died.'

But she continued regarding me intently. Had she seen me somewhere else, I wondered - on local television perhaps, doing my weekly forecasts?

'Well, I hope it is the right Dorothy,' I said, 'because I really don't think I can start again from scratch!'

Suddenly, she brightened. 'I haven't remembered anything else since I spoke to you on the telephone - except that she wore a cloak.'

'A cloak?'

'Yes, that's right. She often wore a long cloak.'

So, Dorothy Browning: A colourful and cultured Christian; not tall, who fraternised with nuns, may have written poetry, always wore a hat - and now a cloak. Well, let's hope it wasn't black, and let's hope it wasn't a pointy hat.

After delivering the Good News to my mother that October evening, I decided that I would examine the chart for the moment I first contacted Mrs Hawes. It turned out to be rather revealing. True, it did show me in the Third House (of telephone calls) but it also mirrored the chart for the moment Eleanor found Dorothy in the parish register. Same angles; Uranus rising and Pluto culminating. Meanwhile - and this is what confirmed it for me – Jupiter, planet of Faith, conjoined the Nadir, the very root of it. This could hardly have been more apt. But did it show where I was headed next?

Astrologers might look askance at the Void of Course Moon in Pisces. Was I about embark on another wild goose chase? Yes. On my next day off, I spent many a happy hour tucked away in the library with my illicit sandwiches, ploughing through back copies of the parish magazine, and reading volume upon volume of religious and romantic verse; but although I did unearth an obscure woman poet named Dorothy Browning whose, 'Castles in the Sand,' rather appealed, the dates didn't fit. Before long, however; and thanks to the fortuitous intervention of my friend Joanna's mother (who had recently completed a degree in English Literature) I was introduced to the works of Peter Baker. M.C. War poet and adventurer.

At last, I thought. Baker had been Dorothy's maiden name. Could he have been a distant relative? It didn't seem unlikely. Her inscription seemed just the sort of thing he may have penned as one of the post-war, 'New

Romantics.' The critic I read didn't think much of them; 'sentimental, derivative and arrogant,' or words to that effect; but I didn't let his judgment put me off, and therefore spent the best part of my October half term, trying to establish a relationship between Dorothy and Peter Baker: - an attempt which brought me into conversation with an archivist at Conservative Party Headquarters; a helpful private secretary, and several elderly Tory ladies in the Southern Shires (one of whom kindly sent me his photograph, which I kept for a while on my bedside table to inspire me in my quest).

Delighted to find that Peter Baker and I shared the same birthday, I pursued him with great zeal - only to discover that he had been arraigned in 1954 on charges of embezzlement, cast out of the Commons and sentenced to eight years in Wormwood Scrubs. He may have escaped from the Gestapo twice and won the Military Cross but he was no match for the representatives of British Justice.

Oh, but I really liked him. It didn't bother me in the least that he had been a reckless adventurer, and alleged misappropriator of funds. It still, however, seemed to bother Conservative Central Office. I found him thanks to one of the obliging Tory Ladies in the Southern shires. The archivist I spoke to couldn't find any trace of him in their records.

Yet another War hero vanishes. Yet another hero fails to receive due recognition. And because I'd got rather fond of *this* Peter – who'd undergone a religious conversion in prison following a Dark Night of the Soul - I was really hoping he would turn out to be the One. Ah, if only. If only I could find a connection between Dorothy and Peter Baker then I would rest content. And, I worked very hard on it, believe you me, reading his entire poetic opus, as well as his prison memoir, 'Time Out of Life,' all in the hope of finding a mention of her name.

He had been a publisher, in one of his many guises. She had been a private secretary in one of hers. Could he have employed her at some point? Could he have learned of her death and commissioned the headstone by way of thanks? It certainly seemed to me the kind of impulsive and generous gesture he would have made. He had been an Aries, with Mars in expansive Sagittarius. His Neptune in Leo exactly conjoined Dorothy's Sun. He may never have met her, but if he had, he would surely have been entranced. But, alas, the longed-for connection did not materialise. The only thing he had in common with Dorothy, as far as I could establish (aside from the shared surname) was that they had both died untimely, aged forty-five.

'My narrator,' I told Bill, when I called round to see him, 'wishes to discover that Peter was a romantic poet with a distinguished War record who was tortured by the Gestapo, once employed Dorothy as his secretary, sympathised with her predicament and admired her literary powers.'

'Oh, yes? And I imagine the Philosopher character wishes he was cat meat.'

'Oh come on, Bill, don't be like that. I thought you'd be pleased.'

'Pleased? I haven't seen hide nor hair of you for the past eight weeks and now you bring me another dead thing. You are unbelievable, Gwendolen, do you know that? The most self-centred woman I have ever met.'

'Well, I don't think that's very fair, Bill. I have called round before now to see how you are, and you haven't been in. Besides, you could always have contacted me.'

'Whatever for?'

'All right, if you're going to be like that, I'll go home – without giving you your present.'

'Now, why would you want to give me a present?'

'To say thank you. For Peter Baker. It was you who conjured him up. You told me a story, remember: whoosh, there he goes, Peter, armed only with his Penguin Book of Romantic Verse. He escapes from the Gestapo and wins the Military Cross.'

At last, a smile. 'A story,' he said. 'To amuse you. I don't think you'll find he'll turn out to be The One. It'll turn out to be one of the Key Players – someone you already know.'

'I think you've found him,' said my mother (this would have been during one of our last phone-calls).

'Do you think so? Do you really think it might be him?'

'Yes, he sounds just like your father to me.'

'Ah, but he's got the same birthday as me – astrologically-speaking. He had the Sun in exactly the same degree of Aries.'

'Well, there you are then: you and your father all rolled into one, a poet and a gambler. You need look no further.'

'Now, Mum, you know very well that I'm like you in many ways. You're a Romantic really, and so am I. And I'm becoming organised. I'm writing everything down now, when I make a find. I've even started a new filing system.'

'I'll believe that when I see it.'

'All right then, I'll bring you my files next time I come.'

'I'd rather you brought me your story. I want to see you finish something. And now you've got this Peter chap and you know it's your father, you've got no excuse!'

'I will finish it,' I said. 'I will. Oh, I do wish you could show some faith in me. I'm your daughter too, not just Dad's and I love you as much as I ever loved him - only differently. I have enormous respect for you!'

She softened. 'You are yourself, Gwendolen, always have been. And a very loving person really. If I've been critical, then I'm sorry. But if I have, it's only because I know what you can do.'

She died on November 23rd, very quickly, in the small hours of the morning. She didn't press her buzzer. She was ready for the off. Uranus returned to its natal place. Bill came round. Mum went out.

It was Eleanor who woke before the telephone rang and called out her name: Eleanor who wrote the words for her inscription: 'Marigolds and Daisies Forever in Your Heart.'

'The dawn of life awoken, a tiny little seed; forever growing; nothing to need.'

Eleanor, the poet: my mother's dream: her
Peter.

CHIRON

Although I had promised my mother that I would finish Dorothy's story, after her death I put my research on hold: I was too unhappy to write and too busy sorting through her effects. We spent Christmas with Bill's sisters in Yorkshire and the New Year with my brother; then there was work to be done on the house, then Spring Cleaning. I hadn't forgotten, but my plan was to take a year out from teaching and get on with it then. Dorothy, however, didn't seem too keen on this schedule, or so it appeared, for towards the end of the Summer Term I received another prompt; this time loud and clear.

It happened this way.

I was coming to the end of a typical teaching day when I had to cover a Drama lesson for an absent colleague: not a prospect I relished, Year 8 Drama last thing in the afternoon. Wasn't it just my luck, I thought, to get a cover in my last free lesson of the year; and I trudged over to the Drama Studio after picking up a book from the library, feeling very hard done by and in no mood for anything theatrical.

Fortunately, work had been set. I quickly scanned the instructions, silenced the class and told them what they had to do. Their task was to 'Create a Character,' and this character had to have some kind of quirk. Fair enough, I thought. I could probably cope with that. So, after explaining what a quirk was, I sent them off to get on with it, and sat down in a far corner to read; calling them back into the circle towards the end of the lesson so they could introduce their characters to their peers.

All went smoothly. And, predictably enough, their characters all had trendy modern names, mainly after celebrities; worked in some glamorous occupation, and adopted various quirky modern habits none of which I can recall. Except for one.

A girl stood up. I can see her now: confident and clear-eyed; fair-haired, pretty. She looked directly at me and said: 'My character's named Dorothy. She's forty-five and a housewife and her quirk is cleaning.'

A jolt – something electric – went straight through me.

'What?' I stammered. 'What do you mean, cleaning, that's not a quirk.'

'Yes it is.'

'But everybody cleans.'

'Her quirk is cleaning,' she repeated firmly.

'Do you mean she had some sort of obsession with cleaning? Some kind of compulsion, like people who keep washing their hands or checking the plugs?'

'That's right,' she replied, and sat back down. She'd had enough, but I persisted: 'It's rather an old-fashioned name, isn't it, Dorothy? Is it a family name?'

'No.'

'I was just wondering where you got the name from.'

She shrugged. 'It just came.'

'Just like that?'

'Yes,' she replied, exchanging a look half way between pity and bemusement with her neighbour.

By now, the class were becoming restless so I quickly moved them on, but I was badly shaken, I can tell you. I just wanted the lesson to end so that I could get home as quickly as possible and lie down. This was too much, even for me; and, for a while, I wandered around the car park in a complete daze. I felt as though I were walking on a bouncy castle, or a carpet which had captured a pocket of air, and I've got no idea how I managed to drive home. But I do remember - very clearly - that it was only after I had managed to calm down and went to draw the chart for this 'event' that I noticed the date: Wednesday, July 11th 2001. It was Dorothy's anniversary - and I had forgotten.

'A coincidence,' said Bill over dinner. 'A disturbing one, I'll grant you, but a coincidence nonetheless. Or there is bound to be a rational explanation.'

Something in his tone of voice annoyed me and I snapped back. 'Why? Why do we always have to a rational explanation? Why can't we have an irrational one – for once?'

'Because that wouldn't be an explanation,' he replied, dipping a chunk of bread in the left-over pasta sauce. 'Do you want to look at this – or not?'

'Yes, all right then.'

'Very well. The most likely explanation is that you will have met this class before and forgotten. After all, you've only got to meet someone once and you're telling them all about Dorothy and your research. I'm amazed, actually, that she doesn't get more visitors. Then again, the girl could just as easily have overheard you telling someone else.'

'And remembered the details?' I put in. 'She got her name, age, occupation – and all on the anniversary of Dorothy's death. Oh, I could have covered the class before and forgotten, that's certainly possible, but do you really think the average thirteen year old pays any attention whatsoever to teachers in cover lessons because I don't.'

'But you are hardly the average teacher as you know.'

'Yes, we're talking here about the average thirteen year old. They've got better things to do with their time than memorise details of teacher's conversations; or their research projects, for that matter.'

He shrugged, 'I still think she was winding you up. Kids do that. I used to wind my teachers up, didn't you?'

'No, I didn't, actually. I was very well behaved as a child on the whole. Oh, I used to argue, but I would come straight out with it. I was never a winder-upper. But never mind me, Bill. There was nothing in this girl's manner to suggest a wind up. She was very direct. If anything she seemed irritated and didn't like me bothering her. She'd done the work, she gave straight answers - and there I was bothering her with a lot of silly questions. Her whole manner seemed to say: 'Get a life, Miss.' No, I've been teaching twenty years, I know a wind up when I see one.'

'In that case, what we are looking at is simply coincidence. You're especially alert to these, as we know. You pick up on things other people would ignore because that's what you're like, you set these things up.'

'Oh, I set it up did I, for my colleague to be absent? Not only that, I set the work he left. I then set it up to give myself the Drama Cover. What a helpful little History teacher I am. Well, if I'm setting cover these days, perhaps I should ask them to pay me for it. That'd go down well on Top Corridor!'

'You know very well that I did not mean you set the lesson, although I am sure you would rather believe it was all Discarnate Dorothy's doing. That cannot have happened. What does happen is that you set it up for us to have these arguments. You ask me for explanations, which you don't really want and then you argue. You're not interested in what I think.'

'Yes, I am,' I replied. 'I'm always interested in other viewpoints.'

'But you've already decided that you think.'

'No, I haven't. If I'd already decided, I wouldn't get into a flap when these things happen. I'm just trying to work things out.'

'All right,' he said, pushing away his plate and reaching for his cigarettes. 'You're looking for explanations, you say. Well, there are explanations outside the Medieval Mystical World View. At my end, you ask for these but don't listen. You ask me for explanations then tell me I'm wrong.'

'No, I don't.'

'Yes, you do.'

'Well, you tell me I'm wrong.'

He inhaled sharply. 'I do not. I do not say, 'you are wrong,' which is what you do all the time.'

'Well, I do think you're wrong to say that there is no God; and this is all there is to it; this life. So you're right. I do think you're wrong about that. But perhaps you can understand how, when I hear you tell me, 'that cannot have happened,' I hear you telling me I'm wrong.'

'No, that's not what I'm saying. That is not what I mean.'

'But you think I am wrong.'

'I think you are mistaken – it's not the same thing.'

'Well, I'm sorry, Bill, but it sounds the same to me.'

'Because you don't listen. I tell you; you're not, actually, interested in what I think.'

'I'm not interested in thinking like you. I am interested in what you think because I'm interested in you as a person. I'm interested in your story. I'm just not interested in adopting your philosophy - or anyone else's. As for my own, I know there's more to life than meets the eye, I just haven't sorted it out yet. I'm still working on it.'

'You're working on the details but you have already decided on the bigger picture.'

'Oh, have I?'

'I think you have. But let's see. You say you haven't decided? '

'That's right.' I cut into a nectarine.

'But, so far, you think everything's connected. Nothing happens by chance. Is that what you believe?'

'I do feel that everything is connected in some mysterious way, and that life is purposeful, meaningful, yes. I just don't know what it is.'

'All right then. So, according to your own beliefs; the Cosmos will have sent you me for a purpose. Everything is connected. Well, here you are. And here I am. The Cosmos has sent you me. You are looking for a philosophy to underpin your Astrology. I'm a Philosopher. I've considered these questions long and hard. I could give you explanations. Here's one. Let's try this one on. If Astrology works, it's because that's the way the Universe is structured. No more, no less. No other agency involved. But you wouldn't be interested in that because you have already decided. You say you haven't but you have.'

'I decided long ago that I would decide for myself.'

'Yes, quite right. That's how it should be. And all very admirable. But when you have an opportunity to do so, you don't actually listen. You think you do but you don't. And, you know, it isn't me who starts this, it's you.'

Was he right? I knew I could be argumentative, but was it correct that I didn't listen? I felt that I had been but, by now, I was drifting away and eating my nectarine. I was looking towards the window and thinking. Perhaps the Cosmos sent me Bill for some other purpose? Perhaps the Cosmos hadn't sent him at all? In fact, I had put an ad' in 'Private Eye.'

Having exhausted Bill as a source of rational explanation that evening, I decided to try my luck with the Astrology Group, presenting the chart for this latest episode as a mystery chart. And the chart - as I had drawn it - certainly mystified the Astrologers - to a woman. What on earth was I doing, they wanted to know, leaving all the planets symbolising myself out of the picture?

It was Moira who spotted this: 'Where's Mars?' she demanded. 'And where's Pluto? Both your rulers, you've left them out.'

'You weren't there,' quipped Cassie.

Wincing, I passed my hand along the back of my neck which felt clammy and hot. 'I, I just slipped up.'

'A Freudian slip?'

'Sorry?'

'A Freudian slip,' she repeated. 'An act of self-forgetting. So, what were you doing in the lesson, before the children presented their drama? Can you remember?'

I could, of course. I'd been reading a psychology book, which had brought back a memory from childhood I preferred to forget, and certainly didn't wish to disclose, so I lied. 'Nothing. I just sat down in a corner, and marked a couple of exercise books.'

'You didn't fall asleep?'

'No! You don't fall asleep in a lesson full of children doing Drama. What is this, Cassie, the Spanish Inquisition? Really, I was just sitting there not doing anything apart from my job.'

Sensing my discomfiture, Evelyn moved in to protect me, I suspect. 'Yes, I'm not sure that every slip is a Freudian slip,' she said kindly. 'But perhaps we can move on to another chart now. Gwendolen, would you mind?'

'Not at all.'

Fortunately, Annie had brought one. I have no idea what it was about because I spent the next twenty minutes fighting off anxiety. But I knew I wouldn't be able to keep it up so during the next tea break, I made my excuses to Evelyn who rose to see me out. 'I'm sorry that you felt under pressure this evening,' she added at the front door, 'but if you want to talk, I hope you'll feel you can.'

She knows, I thought as I climbed into my car and lit a cigarette, but then I thought; why would she? I hadn't even told my mother. No, of course, she didn't know. No need to start thinking along those lines. No need to go back there. It was just a coincidence; that was all, me leaving myself out of the chart. It didn't mean anything. Oh, but what on earth had possessed me to pick a bloody psychology book, I'd have been better off with Enid Blyton. Yes, that was my favourite, the Wishing Chair. And as I drove home, I went back through all my favourite childhood stories; repeating their titles again and again: the stories I read, and the ones my mother told me. But the story I had told myself kept coming back. Try as I might, I couldn't push it back down. I was a good person. I looked after my father. I was his Little Eyes. It didn't matter what the babysitter did to my body. She couldn't hurt me the real me. I wasn't there.

When I got home, I did ring Evelyn. 'Bill said I tried to carve out for him a Land Fit for Heroes. I did try. I wanted it to be pure. I wanted it to be beautiful. How could I tell him when things weren't so good? My father alone in the dark in the next room. How could tell him? I wanted it to be beautiful. I did try.'

'Of course you did,' she said. 'You loved him.'

'It's not going to happen again,' I told Dorothy, calling round the following morning after a night of no sleep. 'It's not going to happen again because I've had enough now. And don't think I haven't spotted what you've been up to. July 11th, indeed. Oh, I'm sorry. I forgot your anniversary. It's also mine.

Ping, and all the lights went on in Blackpool. Ping, and I made the decision to incarnate. Ping and my mother reached for her Good Housekeeping Diary. And all on the anniversary of your death.

Oh, but I should take my hat off to you, Dorothy. What a wonderful sense of humour you've got. Aren't you the joker in the pack? Ah, but you can't hide behind humour any more. I know exactly what you've been up to. And how do I know? Because I'm now looking in a mirror. Oh, I've struggled to see myself at times, but I can see you clear as daylight. I can see how you've been in my life. You've been trying to save me. You've been trying to shine your light on poor old me. Yes, that's you, Dorothy, a real saviour- redeemer. Well it isn't working and it's got to stop because I've had enough now. I don't want any more prompts. I'm not up to it.

It's all right for you - you've got someone to fall back on because you trust God. Well I don't. And it is any wonder?

Oh, I trust my charts, I trust my signs, but I don't trust God who made the Stars for Signs, and that's the bottom line.

Ah, but you do, Dorothy. Yes, you do. So, will you please ask God to let me off the hook now, please, because I've had enough now? Get him to sack me.

Oh? I could let it go, could I?

After all this time?

I could, could I?

Well, don't wait up.'

Yes, well, perhaps I should have known better than to have thrown down the gauntlet quite so dramatically, because things happened very quickly after that. When I got home, I went straight to my files, intending to burn the lot. Charts, certificates, notebooks, diaries, letters, could all go on the pyre. And so could my mother's Good Housekeeping diaries. But as I tipped them from the box, I found the one for the last year of her life. And opened it. And saw her practice handwriting. How she had tried to teach herself to write with her left hand after the stroke. And I couldn't do it.

'All right, Mum,' I said, 'I'll give it another go. One more for the road.'

So, when I returned from my holiday in France, I resumed my quest, and managed to track down a living relative: not of Dorothy, of Edith Pook, widow. And yes, you've guessed it: he turned out to be another vicar (albeit retired).

Bill appreciated my dilemma.

'Yes, I can see your problem - when you ring him up out of the blue saying, 'Good Morning, Reverend, I'm an astrologer and I'm strangely interested in your late-lamented aunt.'

I followed him into the kitchen and picked up one of my cats.

'I doubt I'll put it quite like that.'

'I doubt you'll put it any way at all,' he replied, popping a milky coffee into the microwave. 'You won't do it, not now it's come to the crunch. Too risky.'

'You're sure about that, are you?'

'Not a hundred per cent, no, but that's my guess. Of course, they stopped burning women like you years ago - thanks to the Enlightenment.'

'Yes, but there's still a stigma against Astrology. They say it works because the Devil works.'

'Is that what they say? I'm surprised they can't do better than that.'

'They forget the Magi who followed the Star. They were Astrologers.'

'Which didn't happen.'

'Yes, it did.'

'Because it says so in the Bible?'

'No, the Star was there.'

'Oh, well, of course, you're a Christian.'

'No, I'm not.'

'You're a closet Christian, always have been. It's in your background. For all your talk of cosmic energies and the like, you're still a dualist. If I believed in Reincarnation - which I don't - I'd say you were still a Cathar.'

At this point, the microwave pinged - a sign that his coffee had boiled over.

'Damn,' he said, then filled another mug for a fresh attempt. 'Yes, but you won't go there either will you? You keep going back to the Pyrenees. But you never go there, to Montsegur. And you won't go after Peter, either, not now it's come to the crunch. You don't want to meet your God.'

'That's not true,' I said, 'and I will go after Peter.'

'There's the 'phone.'

I didn't move.

He nodded sagely. 'Of course, there is an alternative. There always is. You could choose to look at your experience in the Drama lesson differently. Dorothy was giving you permission to invent him. Create a Character, wasn't that the theme? Yes, go ahead, Gwendolen, she said: make him up; it's all the same to me. But you won't do that either, not if I'm any judge, because you're still looking for some Absolute Truth which you hope is out there. Still hoping you'll get it right. So you won't invent him. And you won't 'phone the vicar either. So you're stuck, aren't you?'

I had to admit it: I was.

So, did I finally move on it because Bill, too, doubted me? No, though I'm sure he helped. In the end, I consulted the Cosmos.

The chart contained a Mutual Reception which indicates choice. I could make the reception, or I could leave it alone. But to make the reception, I would have to imagine the Moon changing places with Jupiter. I would have to bring Jupiter into my house. So I did it. I rang the vicar. I rang him because, after all this time, I wanted the truth. And if it turned out there was no Peter, I would simply say so: it wouldn't be much of an ending, but it would be the truth.

The message I got in the Drama Lesson that day had nothing to do with Peter. Create a Character?

Yes, she meant me.

Was it a coincidence that I had been feeling martyred on that occasion?

Was it mere coincidence that I had been stricken in my hands and feet?

Was it just coincidence that my skin cracked open on July 11th, 1999?

No!

Create a Character?

She meant me!

VENUS HESPERUS

As I begin this chapter, Mercury and Venus combine in the sky, performing an elegant duet in graceful, balanced Libra – which is a bit of a shame, really, since elegant duets are not my style. Perhaps I should wait until Venus collides with Mars, clashes with Uranus or dissolves under Neptune, then we could all enjoy plenty of fireworks and shocking revelations from a mystical perspective or on the Astral Plane. It's tempting. It really is. But then I don't want to postpone things indefinitely. In fact, I don't want to postpone them at all. So let's take advantage of this combination and have some fun with names.

The name Dorothy means, 'Gift of God,' I believe, or, 'Beloved of God,' while her middle name, 'Margaret' means 'Pearl.' I always thought Dorothy a beautiful name. I had an aunt by marriage called Dorothy of whom I was very fond; and my father's favourite sister (who also died young) was named Margaret. So Dorothy Margaret was already a magical name for me.

'Taffy' I originally thought meant Welsh. This was my mother's nickname given by the troops she nursed during the War, and I was born on the River Taff. After discovering, however, that Dorothy was born in Oxford, I decided it was probably onomatopoeic and, very likely, given by a child; possibly a younger sibling: Dorothy, Doffy, Daffy, Taffy....

My own name, Gwendolen, means, 'White Circle,' although my mother didn't choose it in the hope that I may one day start my own coven: she actually named me Gwendolen because, 'the Importance of Being Ernest,' was her favourite play. Not that I'm complaining. It could have been worse. I could have been a lot worse, considering that she went into labour during an attack of acute wind. No, Gwendolen, although hardly enigmatic, is probably an improvement on Flatulence, and definitely an improvement on:

'Small-person-without-any-manners-who-ought-to-be-spanked.'

Which is what 'Taffy' means – as I discovered on October 28th, at 4.15 a.m.

I had been writing well into the small hours when I got up from the floor to reach for my dictionary. Now, I am not sure how this happened. I suppose I must have dislodged it, but another book fell down from the shelf and landed in my hearth, open on page 100. I picked it up and read:

'And his little girl daughter's name was Taffimai Metallumai, and that means; Small-person-without-any-manners-who-ought-to-be-spanked,' – But I am going to call her Taffy. And she was Tegumai

Bopsulai's Best Beloved and her own Mummy's Best Beloved, and she was not spanked half as much as was good for her.'

Well, not according to Rudyard Kipling she wasn't. As for me (O Best Beloved) I don't believe in spanking children (or anyone else for that matter) as neither did my mother: who-herself-was-never-spanked-as-a-child. Well, not by: She-who-always-wore-a-hearing-aid-and-alarmed-the-neighbours-with-her-strange-forebodings-of-impending-disaster.

We may have been Welsh, but we weren't Neanderthals.

Unlike Taffy: the inventive little Daddy's Girl in Kipling's, 'The First Letter,' who much preferred going off with her father fishing to sitting round the cooking pot back home with the rest of the tribe.

She must have been an Aries.

And Tegumai Bopsulai?

That means: 'Man-who-does-not-put-his-foot-forward-in-a-hurry.'

A Taurus, in other words.

I smiled.

'Small-person-without-any-manners-who-ought-to-be-spanked.'

Wonderful!

'Man-who-does-not-put-his-foot-forward-in-a-hurry.'

And began to laugh. Yes, that was my Dad, all right!

By now, I was laughing so much I rolled off the sofa. I let the book drop; rolled off the sofa and rolled around on the floor; clutching my sides and giving myself a stitch through laughing. It might not strike you as particularly funny, but I found it hilarious; and, at one point, had to leave the house in case I woke Eleanor. I drove to the all night Tesco, bought a large bag of doughnuts, then came home and burst out laughing again. Really, I don't think I've laughed so much since my father died. In fact, I know I haven't. Good job I'm not incontinent (yet).

When I finally calmed down, I read the story again: and loved it – because it was Taffy, you see, who invented the first letter of the Alphabet. Created a character, in other words. That's what she did in the story. She created a character, *literally*.

In the story, she drew a picture, only her tribe misunderstood it and all sorts of havoc ensued; but, happily, it all worked out 'Just So' in the end. She then went on to invent the Alphabet (despite being female).

Well, I thought, how come I didn't spot this before? I've had that book on my shelves all along. Trouble was, I'd never read it. Kipling was out of favour when I was a child. Not part of my cultural heritage. But he would have been part of Edwardian Dorothy's – and my mother's. I expect the book had been one of hers. Or she had given it to Eleanor – who hadn't read it either. In fact, judging by its pristine condition, it hadn't been read by anyone in our household.

I smiled, remembering my mother. I could just see her, sitting on an astral park bench with her Wartime Love, Jimmy - and looking very pleased with herself:

'That's my daughter down there, Jim, I expect she thinks it's all her doing but if it hadn't been for me leaving that book behind…..'

From Bill, a sardonic smile. 'You make these things happen. You set them up.'

Not to mention Richard: 'Now, Gwendolen, you have always lived in stories. You have a Mercury Karma: Mercury conjunct the Node.'

And Dorothy, 'Taffy,' Browning?

I imagine she loved every minute of it. What do you think (O Best Beloved)?

For me, the best part was this. Although her tribe didn't understand her pictures, she held fast to her vision, did young Taffy. She stamped her foot (rather a lot, actually) and never wavered. She trusted her own vision. Indeed, she never doubted it. So that was the best part of it all for me because my tribe didn't understand my pictures either - only I did not hold fast to my own vision. I let it go.

I saw my dead grandfather sitting on a swing in the park where I played as a child; a priest standing guard outside the Archbishop's House next door, the night he fell critically ill. I saw quite a few dead people, actually, when I was a child, but I wasn't believed. Oh, don't get me wrong: I was never punished. I had a vivid imagination, I was told, which was all very well, but it was only invention. So, after a while I grew to doubt it. I lost confidence in my vision, which meant that the night my father died, I was struck by a deadly grief: for I no longer trusted my own vision. I had forgotten. Or perhaps I had never believed it was truly mine.

'Good morning, Taffy,' I said when I called round at daybreak. 'What else can I say apart from thank you and would you like a doughnut? I was about to say you have no idea what this means to me, but, of course, you have. Whoever you are, you have surely been a Godsend to me.'

I then tidied up on the grave for a while, then came home and cleaned my house in preparation for a celebration. The women of Mercury Phosphorus were going to get Peter, at long last.

Peter?

Yes, you know: 'to you the stars, narcissi fields and music.' Peter.

I already knew by then, of course, who Peter was. The vicar told me. But I've been keeping it under my hat. Oh, but you'll want Peter first, I suppose. Oh, all right then, fair enough. Not a soldier, not a stalker, not her husband, lover, priest. Ever heard of Peter Pook?

Oh, surely not, I hear you saying; surely Beloved Dorothy wasn't carrying on an affair with Edith's husband, Peter Pook?

'No, that's right, she wasn't. Edith's husband was named William. Peter was the nickname he gave his wife - as I had found out when I rang her nephew: -

'Yes,' he'd said, chuckling, 'that's exactly the kind of thing she used to write in her letters. It was her nickname, given to her by my uncle. They all called her Peter in their circle. You know, Peter Pook.'

Well of course, I didn't know. I'd never heard of Peter Pook. But I didn't want to sound ignorant, so I said, 'Oh, yes, of course. Peter Pook. Ha, ha.'

So, there you have him. Or, rather her. And here they are both: *Dorothy Browning. Taffy. July 11th 1946. To you the stars, narcissi fields and music. Peter (Pook)*

'I like it,' said Annie, breaking the silence. 'It's not what I was expecting but it's growing on me, I think.'

'Yes, I rather like it too,' said Evelyn.

'Well, I don't like at all,' said Cassie. 'It all sounds very dodgy to me.'

'Are you absolutely sure?' Daphne asked.

'Positive,' I replied. 'Peter was definitely Edith – Edith Pook. Now, I'm not sure why her husband gave her that nickname. There's a book by Kipling, 'Puck of Pook's Hill,' but the children in that are called Dan and Una, so maybe it was a private joke. Then again, it may have been descriptive of her character. She dabbled in painting and writing verse, and her nephew described her as rather fey. 'It's not a word we use much nowadays, is it,' he said, 'fey?' Did I know what it meant? Oh yes, I replied, I know the meaning of fey.'

'You certainly do,' said Moira, resuming her knitting. 'Yes, very puckish – the whole thing.'

'Yes, indeed,' said Evelyn. 'But I must say, Gwendolen, I'm sorry we didn't spot it when you showed us your Horary Chart. I'm afraid none of us saw that coming.'

'Oh, I did.' Annie reached for another slice of Victoria sponge. 'I remember now. Uranus in Aquarius in the Seventh. I told Gwen she was in for a shock, and she got one. And, of course, Edith was an Aquarius. Same as me.'

But Cassie still had reservations: 'I wouldn't be too happy about my husband's mistress writing the inscription on my headstone. If anything would bring me back, that would. How can you be sure that's not what you were meant to find out?'

'She wasn't his mistress,' I replied.

'They lived together didn't they?'

'Not while Dorothy was alive.'

'So when did Edith's husband die?'

'After Dorothy: 1949. Really, Cassie, there wasn't any funny business going on. Well, not that kind of funny business. Edith and Dorothy were friends. Their husbands fought together during the War, which was how they got to know each other. They kept up after the War and their wives became friends.'

'Yes, I can understand it,' said Moira. 'And they understood platonic love in those days. I should think they came to some sort of arrangement between friends. Dorothy knew she was dying so she asked Edith to keep an eye on Wilfrid after she was gone.'

'Or,' said Cassie, deploying her Scorpio again, 'it was the only way she was going to see her name in print. She couldn't get her poems published. Oh, well, she thought, my mate, Dorothy won't mind.'

Eleanor, for some reason, found this highly amusing. 'I always told Mum,' she said. 'I always told her Peter would turn out to be Dorothy's friend.'

This earned her a round of applause.

'So, what do you make of it now?' Evelyn asked when we were alone in the kitchen. 'Are you happy with it?'

'I am. It was well done.'

'And Bill?'

'Oh, he said he already knew.'

'He didn't, though, did he?'

'Well, he did in a way,' I replied. 'He did say it would turn out to be one of the Key Players – someone I already knew. But he didn't tell me it would turn out to be a woman!'

'Now, who could have predicted that?'

Looking back, it seems my brother came closest to the truth when he suggested that Dorothy probably wrote the inscription herself and got one of her, 'wacky women friends,' to make sure it was done - only the friend, being, 'arty and impractical,' got the date wrong - while poor old

Wilfrid footed the bill and didn't even get a mention. Whether this was the case, whether Wilfrid footed the bill, or had anything to do with the inscription whatsoever, I was never able to discover. For me, he remains a shadowy figure and I was never able to track down any of his paintings. Indeed, after speaking to Edith's nephew, I came to doubt that he had painted at all. As far as he had been aware, Browning, as he called him, had made detailed, intricate pen and ink drawings of insects, which were very good, very accurate. Not that he could vouch for their quality personally, because he hadn't seen any of his drawings either, in the days when he had visited his aunt. He had the impression he may have been Royal Academy, but he couldn't be sure. I didn't follow this up. I felt I had come to the end of my search. Wilfrid Browning began his working life as an artist, fought in the trenches, came home, made intricate drawings of insects and ended his days as a security guard at Her Majesty's Treasury. Edith looked after him because she was loyal.

During the last years of her life, Dorothy Browning may – or may not – have returned to Oxford to visit the nuns who shared a house on Magdalen Road. She did return to the churchyard where her father, too, lies buried.

Edith - no, Peter - died in 1972. It wouldn't have been too long after this, I imagine, that Dorothy's grave fell into a state of neglect until I, while wandering, stopped there, lifted my foot and entered another world: my story beginning as hers had ended with Neptune at the point of the grave.

Do stories ever end? I doubt it.

I now know the reason I found Dorothy's grave and although I still can't remember the date, it no longer matters. It wouldn't have been too long after my father died. I found Dorothy's grave because I needed to see for myself and trust my own vision. I needed to see how I had been hurting myself and let it go. And the beauty of it is this: now that I trust my own vision, I no longer feel so alone or afraid. My skin has cleared up, my health has improved, and I look forward to my 45th birthday feeling stronger than I have ever felt. I was looking for a friend that day. I found one, thank God.

EPILOGUE

After I finished my book, I made various attempts to find a publisher only to be told that the relationship between the Astrologer and the Philosopher wasn't properly resolved, which amused Bill no end.

'Confirmation,' he said. 'Confirmation from the World of Publishing!' (This will have been during one of our 'off' periods.)

During our 'on' periods, he would nag me to do something about it. 'You can't just accept rejection from two publishers;' or: 'How many publishers did J.K. Rowling send Harry Potter to? Twelve.' Or even: 'Your mother would be disappointed.'

But I didn't think my mother would be disappointed. True, I hadn't heard from her of late, but I didn't suppose she was occupying her time in the Afterlife, worrying about my failure to find a literary agent. Besides, I wasn't sure I wanted to 'resolve' the relationship with the Philosopher. I rather liked it the way it was. So, after a while, I packed up my manuscript, wrapped it in tissue paper, and put it in the cupboard under the stairs. And there it remained, gathering dust, over the passing years and through all our comings and goings: - through Eleanor leaving home, Bill selling his house, my brother returning to Oxford; me mending Bill's socks, sending him packing, opening the door again.

Now, I can't be sure when this pattern changed because, by then, I'd abandoned all efforts to be organised and no longer kept a diary. So, you will understand, I'm sure, if the rest reads rather hazy.

We were in an 'off' phase when I received a phone-call from the Receptionist at Bill's Surgery, which annoyed me. Clearly he hadn't informed them he'd removed to College rooms. Well, I thought, I'm not his private secretary, and pushed away worrying thoughts. Yet, overnight, they resurfaced, so that when his sister rang the next morning, I already knew. The next thing I remember, I was standing beside my cat at the Vet's, watching her slip away, when my mobile rang. It was Bill's sister, calling from the hospital. The tests had come through: nothing could be done. Eleanor drove back from London, made me a cup of tea, and we buried Spinchey in the garden.

'I don't think this is a very good sign,' I told her. 'She's gone on ahead of him.'

'I don't think so, Mum. They didn't get on.'

'Oh, yes, that's true.'

The next evening, I visited Bill in hospital where he gave me a list of instructions. I can't remember what was on it, but I have a very sharp memory of the look on his face as he leaned forward and grasped my wrist, pressing it into me: 'You are not to mind.'

So, I did as I was told and put my feelings on hold. I even went to France with Eleanor for a week during which time Bill returned to Yorkshire in an ambulance. When I returned, I took the train up and found him holding court in his wheelchair; surrounded by devoted students, his sisters in attendance.

'If you haven't got Leo Ascendant,' I told him, settling down to the night shift, 'I'm a Dutchman.'

He gave a sardonic smile, nodded his head, then nodded off again.

While he slept, I looked around the room for something to read. I had the choice between, 'Fludd,' by Hilary Mantel, and, 'the God Delusion,' by Richard Dawkins, both of which I assumed to have been brought as gifts; the former, I supposed, from one of his sisters; the latter from one of his students, fearing he might recant at the last moment and be lost to the Atheist Cause.

Now, normally I wouldn't read anything by Richard Dawkins who once wrote an article in the Independent entitled, 'The real romance in the stars,' advocating the prosecution of professional astrologers under the Trades Description Act and calling astrology an 'aesthetic affront.'

But it was going to be a very long night so, after reading, 'Fludd,' I turned to, 'the God Delusion.'

'What did you think?' Bill asked me in the morning.

I moved to sit in the chair beside his bed. 'Well, he's no philosopher, is he?'

'He is not.'

'You could have done better.'

'I could.'

'I preferred Fludd. He reminded me of you.'

'Did he indeed?'

'He did. A magician.'

Before I left, I told him I wasn't going to say goodbye.

'No,' he replied. '*We* don't need to have that conversation.'

I had just packed my weekend bag ready for my next visit, and was sitting in my garden on his smoking bench when a cloud passed overhead. I shivered and thought: he's gone.

He went out with the summer when Saturn opposed my Sun.

The following spring, I drove up to Yorkshire to receive my portion of his ashes from his sister (who had divided them up) and we drove round the Dales visiting some of his favourite haunts during which excursion I felt strangely detached.

It seemed to me that, from now on, I would occupy a waiting room in life. The last train had departed. I wasn't on it. But never mind. And in my dreams during this period, I often saw myself standing on the platform at Oakworth Station, watching steam trains passing through. The passengers were heading somewhere, but I didn't envy them or feel any inclination to climb on board. And since I had to wait, I thought, why not move to where the views are better than in Oxford? I might as well have something beautiful to look at. I also needed to release some capital, having taken early retirement from teaching. So, I put my house on the market at Whitsun and found a buyer within a week. He couldn't complete before the autumn, but that suited me fine.

Intending to move to Yorkshire, I placed an offer on a weavers' cottage in the Pennines because I liked the look of the fireplace. It was a great huge fireplace, with a slab of stone on top, so big you could almost move into it. I could be happy here, I thought; I wouldn't have to wash my hair or change my clothes and no one would be any the wiser, but the vendor changed her mind so I decided to go and live with my brother instead as a stop gap. Eleanor was working abroad at the time so Joanna came up from London the night before to help me move.

We packed throughout the evening, ordered a takeaway curry, and carried on packing for much of the night. In the morning, she nodded towards the glass jar on the mantelpiece which had once contained his favourite Putanesca pasta sauce.

'Are we taking Bill to Bampton, Gwen?'

'I should think so, yes.'

'Only I wouldn't have thought it was his kind of place.'

'No, no; it's a lovely place.'

'Bit rural, though, isn't it, for Bill?'

'No, he liked the countryside. He didn't like to spend too much time in it, but he liked it.'

'All right then. Shall we just leave him where he is for now while we do the kitchen floor?'

'Good idea.'

So, off we went again, scrubbing and mopping, while the removals men filled the van. By mid-morning, we were all done and dusted. The men drove off to store my belongings - just as my solicitor rang to say that key documents had failed to materialise.

'Oh, dear,' I said.

Joanna shook her head in disbelief. 'Which documents are these?'

'I'm not really sure. I could with a cup of coffee, could you?'

By now, of course, we had sent into storage all kitchen equipment, so we decided to go for a brew at the local café which had a reputation for excellent coffee and a variable clientele. Sandwiched between a lettings agency and an off licence, it had been owned by the same proprietor since the early 1970s and the décor hadn't changed since then - as neither had the staff. A white-haired waiter shuffled back and forth on the chequered linoleum floor, while a dapper man wearing a nylon maroon blazer (who could just as easily have been found cutting hair in the barber shop round the corner) operated the hand-pumped Astoria machine.

'This is where I met the Stonemason,' I told Joanna, as she slid warily onto her cracked vinyl seat.

'I thought you met him in the churchyard?'

'Yes, this is where I met him afterwards - on Dorothy's birthday - when Bill said: 'His name is Peter,' and I nearly shot out of my seat. That one, over there.'

Turning her head, she followed my gaze to a corner booth where a middle-aged couple shared a milky coffee beneath a faded mural depicting produce unavailable on the menu: bunches of grapes, thick red peppers and various fruits de mer. 'Well, it's certainly got an air of unreality, this café. So, did you ever hear from the Stonemason again?'

'I did. Didn't I tell you?'

'Not that I recall.'

'Oh. Oh well, I must have forgotten.' Removing my specs, I wiped the lenses in my scarf. 'Yes, I did meet him again: in the churchyard, after I'd finished my book. It was three years to the day, funnily enough, that my mother had her stroke. Richard was with me and the narcissi were in bloom. And just as we were standing there talking about it, the Stonemason appeared. He was walking on the path behind me with a friend and a couple of dogs.'

'Do you think he may have been sleeping rough?' Jo asked.

'I don't know. I did wonder about that, but then again, he may have just been going to a festival. He had a sleeping bag. Anyway, he was glad to see me. He'd been hoping for the chance to meet me again, he said. He wanted me to know why he hadn't restored the headstone. He had tried. The vicar wouldn't let him.'

'I suppose the vicar may have thought it might have been – well- too much for him?'

'He may have done,' I agreed. 'Although he said he couldn't allow it because I wasn't a relative - if he made an exception for me, they'd all be wanting their headstones done up.'

She gave a wry smile then reached for the menu. 'So, how about Madeleine? Any more news of her?'

'Not since she refused to allow their daughter to visit when he was dying. She wasn't having her daughter visiting a dying man.'

'She wasn't his twin then.'

'No.'

When we got back, my buyer was waiting on the pavement. A young Chemistry Fellow with a shock of yellow hair, bouncing with enthusiasm, he couldn't wait to move in.

Joanna placed her hand on my arm as I fished for my keys. 'You can't let him in, Gwen, the money hasn't arrived.'

'It'll be on its way, surely - and he has got all his stuff.'

'Yes, but he can't move in; he hasn't paid for the house.'

So he had to go and sit with his friends in their van. They were still sitting there two hours later, when my solicitor phoned to say it was most unlikely to happen.

'I don't think the house wants me to leave,' I told Joanna. 'Maybe I've made the wrong decision. Maybe I shouldn't be moving at all.'

'No, I'm sure it is the right decision,' she replied. 'And it will happen, don't worry. But maybe not today.'

'I suppose we could sleep here another night, could we? Or go over to Dan's? Oh, but then we'd have to come back.'

'Hmm, how about we go for a walk and have a bit of think? I wouldn't mind a trip to the churchyard.'

'The churchyard? We could do, I suppose.'

'Shall we take Bill?'

'No, I don't think so, Jo. It's too wet.'

'It's only drizzle. And I wouldn't mind seeing Dorothy's grave.'

'Didn't I take you there before?'

'Yes, but that was ages ago. Come on. We can get something to eat on our way back.'

As I reached for my coat, she reached for the jar, labelled, 'BILL.'

'Oh, I'm really not sure,' I said as she opened her bag.

'Why not see how you feel when you get there? You don't have to. Why not play it by ear and see how you feel?'

When I got there, I felt dreadful. I knew Dorothy wasn't there anymore. She was long gone. Promoted, probably. What was the point of leaving Bill on an empty grave? Anyway, I couldn't unscrew the lid.

'He's staying put,' I said firmly; but no sooner had I said this than a light went on in my head: 'Oh. Jo. He was: man-who-does-not-put-his-foot-forward-in-a-hurry.'

She nodded, 'I think that suits him very well.'

'He never went very far afield, did he? Apart from the annual trip to Scotland with his students. He wasn't much of a traveller, was he?'

'Not really.'

'Mind you, we did have a trip to Whitby once. That was when he poisoned me with his cooking!'

'Yes, I remember that.'

'I nearly died.'

'You were certainly very ill.'

'Oh, but we did have a week in France. We stayed in a Presbytery. But could I get him out of doors? Not likely. Except to a café. Oh, but then one night, I can see it now. He brought me out into the garden and took my hand. Look, he said, and pointed skyward. And there it was, the Milky Way. We saw it together, the Milky Way. Yes, we did.'

'Time to let him go now, Gwen,' she said after a while.

This time the lid came off easily. Kneeling down, I made a little dent in the earth, and patted him in. As I stepped off the grave, my mobile rang: the money had arrived. I would be able to move after all.

'I should think that was probably Dorothy's doing,' said Jo, slipping her arm inside mine as we wandered off. And for the first time in quite a while, I actually felt like smiling. 'Yes,' I said, glancing over my shoulder at the headstone. 'Yes, I should think it was.'

That evening, in my brother's cottage, I sat before the log-burning stove, and cast a final horoscope. Sagittarius rises and Mercury culminates. A Philosopher takes flight and a story sees the light of day.

****

ASTROLOGICAL DATA

All charts calculated for Oxford, UK.

Further information www.ToYoutheStars.co.uk

Neptune: 24/7/1999. 9.01 p.m.

Pluto: 22/9/1999. 5.37 p.m.

Saturn: 28/9 1999. 3.30 p.m.

The Sun: 29/9/1999. 5.07 p.m.

The Moon: Phonecall: 31/10 1999. 7.48 p.m.

Venus Phosphorus: 8/7/2000. 7.58 p.m.

Mars: 6/8/2000. 12.30 p.m.

Mercury: Horary Chart: 10/9/2000. 3.30 a.m.

Uranus: 19/9/ 2000. 4.50 p.m.

Urania: August 6th, 1900 (Time unknown but I had a hunch for about 9.15 a.m.)

Jupiter: Phonecall: 11/10/2000. 4.16. p.m.

Chiron: Drama Lesson: 11/7/2001. 3.01 p.m.

Venus Hesperus: 28/10/ 2001. 4.15 a.m.

Epilogue: 3/10/ 2013. 2.25 p.m.

ACKNOWLEDGEMENTS

To You the Stars is a semi-autobiographical novel based on my research into the life of Dorothy Browning, so I should start by thanking Dorothy for inspiring me while giving equal thanks to my lifelong friend, the writer, Jan Page, without whose encouragement and editorial skills this book would never have seen the light of day.

I would also like to thank Birte Milne and Brenda Page for proof-reading; Emma Jackson Erhard for marketing; Glynis Price, David Kendall, Abigail Hopkins and Hester Ruoff for their contributions to the promotional video, and especially my daughter, Eleanor, for her support and help with research, reading various drafts and filming.

Finally I would like to thank the Pleasant Ladies' Astrology Group for their input and friendship; and last but definitely not least, my 'sparring partner,' the late Bob Hargrave of Balliol College, who gave me the all-important advice that I must let the astrology drive the plot, and the very great gift of understanding.

Wendy Cartwright, 2015.

If you enjoyed reading this novel, please tell your friends, tweet us @toyouthestars, and post a review on Amazon.

For more information about the book and author visit our website: www.toyouthestars.co.uk or our Facebook page: facebook.com/toyouthestars.

Printed in Great Britain
by Amazon.co.uk, Ltd.,
Marston Gate.